THE DISPLACEMENT

A Novel

Jacob E. Williams

Copyright © 2026 by Jacob E. Williams

ISBN: 979-8-9957004-0-1

All rights reserved. No part of this publication may be reproduced, distributed, or transmitted in any form or by any means without the prior written permission of the publisher.

This is a work of fiction. Names, characters, places, and incidents are either products of the author's imagination, or are used fictitiously. Any resemblance to actual persons, living or dead, or actual events is purely coincidental.

Published by Stillwater Books

First Edition

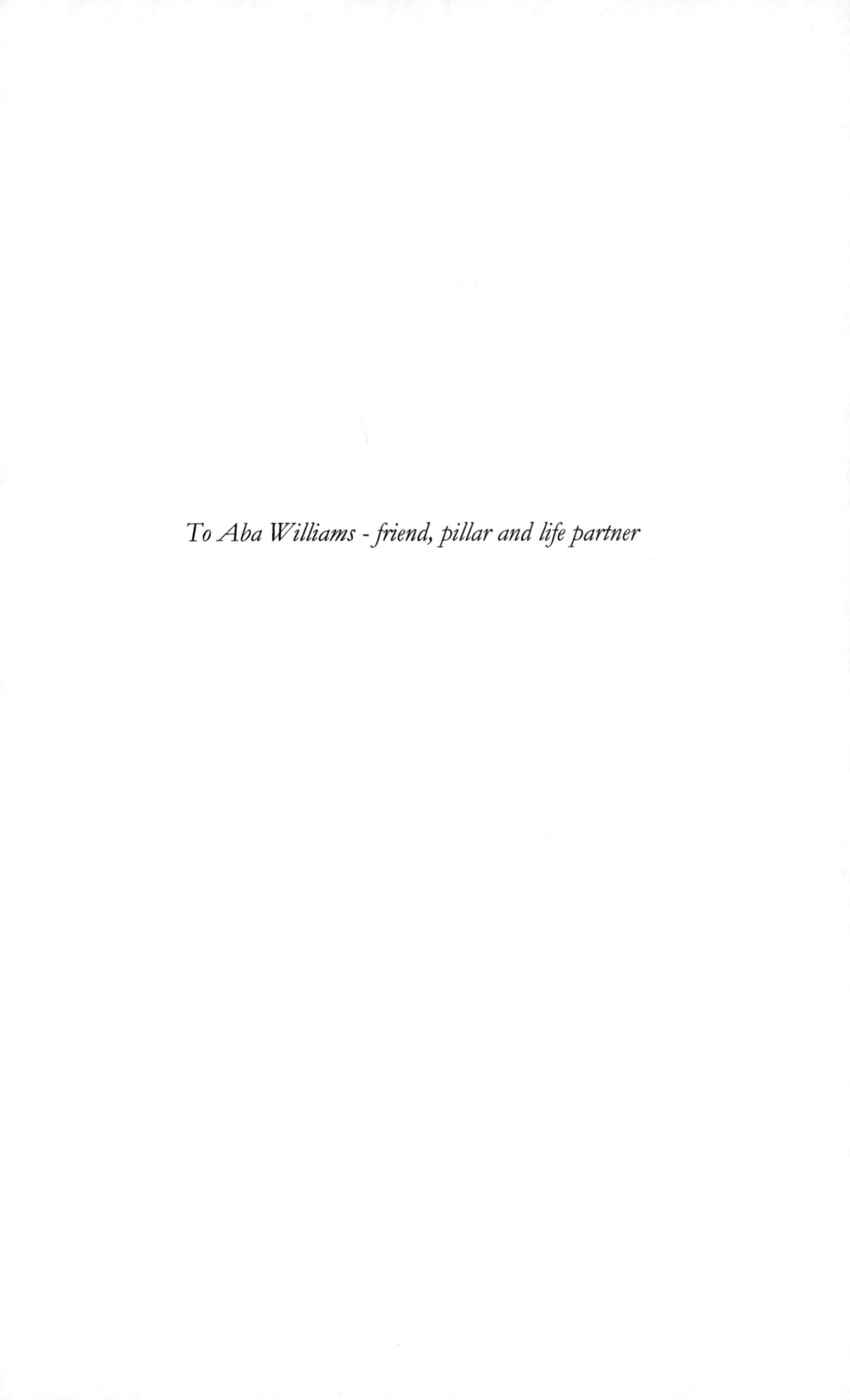

To Aba Williams - friend, pillar and life partner

ACKNOWLEDGEMENT

This book was written in conversation with the world it describes

CONTENTS

PART ONE FRANK

CHAPTER ONE:

Coral Bay, Florida · 2031

The water came in at four in the morning.

Frank knew this because he had not been asleep. He had been lying in the dark waiting for the water, knowing it was coming, uncertain only of how high this third one would climb. The particular sound of water finding the gap beneath the front door was a sound he had catalogued, like so many others, without meaning to. A low susurration, almost polite. The house receiving what it could not stop.

He lay still for a moment after hearing it. Gloria breathed beside him in the familiar rhythm of a woman who had decided, somewhere in her sixties, that she was going to sleep through whatever the night brought, and who mostly succeeded. Frank did not move. He looked at the ceiling and performed the calculations he had been performing since the first flood, seven years ago: the rate of ingress based on the gap dimensions he had measured once and memorized; the overnight rainfall total from the gauge on the back porch, which he checked every evening before bed; the tide chart for the week, which he kept folded in his wallet though he no longer needed to consult it. He knew what the water was going to do. He knew approximately when. He lay in the dark and let the knowledge run its course.

Then he got up, as he always did, and went to meet it.

* * *

By six-thirty the living room held three feet of water and the family was moving.

This was the third time. The first flood had been 2024; they had stood in the kitchen and watched the water enter the house with something close to disbelief, which seemed, in retrospect, remarkable. By the second flood, they had a system. By the third, the system had been refined to the point where it ran almost without coordination, each person knowing their role, no instructions required. Frank observed this as he stood on the deck and watched the water come in off the Gulf. The family machine, operating in the house behind him. His family. His machine.

He could hear Deja through the sliding door: her voice at its particular operational register, which was two degrees flatter than her normal speaking voice and meant she was managing something. Then Isaiah, barely a response, the monosyllable of a fifteen-year-old who had been deployed to a task he found beneath him not because it was unimportant, but because he was somewhere else in his mind and had been for some time. Marcus on the phone; the cadence of a man arguing with an institution, polite and precise and without any real expectation of success.

Gloria he could not hear. Gloria moved in silence when she was working.

Frank turned back to the water.

It was brown at the edges this morning, which meant runoff from the neighborhood rather than clean tidal ingress. Debris in it: a foam cup, a child's sandal, the lid of something. The Gulf itself, half a mile out, was still blue-gray and flat under the overcast. The barrier islands were there, doing what barrier islands did, which was less, and less. Frank had written a section on barrier island degradation rates in the 2019 report. Four pages, footnoted. He could still recite the median projections for St. George Island from memory, the way a man might remember lines of poetry he had not chosen to memorize but had absorbed by proximity over a long enough period.

His hand found the railing without his directing it. His hand had been finding this railing for twenty-three years, since they had built the deck the summer Deja turned twenty. He pressed his palm flat against the wood and felt the familiar slight give of boards that had been wet and dried and wet again across two decades. The house was not falling down. That was the thing people didn't understand, who had not read the report or lived through three floods: the house was not falling down. The water came in and the water went out and the house stood. The damage was cumulative and mostly invisible and the house stood. That was the thing. The disaster was not an event. It was a rate, or something like a rate; he had never found a better word for it.

* * *

He heard the sliding door open behind him.

Deja appeared at his shoulder. She did not come to the railing. She stood a few feet back, the way she had when she was a girl and he had been standing somewhere she wasn't sure she was allowed to approach, and Frank recognized the distance and said nothing about it.

"Car needs to move," she said.

"Isaiah's doing it."

"I know. I meant yours."

Frank's car was in the second bay of the garage, which flooded from the back when the water reached a certain level. He knew the level. He tracked it. He had moved the car before the water reached it in the last two floods and he would move it again.

"I'll move it," he said.

Deja stayed where she was for a moment. He could feel her looking at him in the way she looked at him now, which was the way you looked at something you were trying to read without letting it know you were reading it. His daughter the structural engineer. She understood load-bearing things.

"The Hendersons left," she said. "Truck was gone when I looked this morning."

"I know."

"That's four families on this block since last year."

Frank said nothing.

"Dad."

"I'll move the car, Deja."

Another moment. Then he heard her go back inside.

He stood at the railing and watched the water move across the lawn. It was not rushing. It had no urgency. It did not want anything. It was water behaving as water behaved when there was nowhere else for it to go, finding the level, occupying the space available. Frank had spent thirty years explaining to people, in various professional contexts and with various degrees of success, that the water did not want anything. The water was not coming for them. The water was simply there, and would be more there tomorrow, and more again the year after. People found this harder to hear than they found warnings about storms, because storms had a grammar people understood: they came and they passed and you assessed the damage and you went on. What Frank had spent his career describing was something without that grammar. Something that did not pass.

He looked at the waterline on the second deck post. He had marked the high-water levels on that post with a pencil line each flood, low on the wood, a private record nobody else knew to look for. Three lines now. Each one higher than the last. The distance between the second and third was larger than the distance between the first and second.

The rate was not constant. The rate was increasing.

He had written that sentence, in different language, on page seventeen of the 2019 report. He had also written it on page thirty-one, in the executive summary, in plain English rather than technical register, because he had understood even then that the report would need to speak to people who did not read tables. He had been wrong about who would read it, as it turned out. Nobody had read it. Or nobody had read it in the way he had intended, which was as an instruction.

He took his hand off the railing and went to move the car.

* * *

The garage was dry.

He had built the drainage channel along its back wall himself, ten years ago, the summer after the first serious tidal surge, before the floods were officially floods. He had done it on a Saturday while Gloria was visiting her sister in Tallahassee, which he recognized now, with the clarity of retrospect, as a significant detail. He had not told her why he was building it. He had said he was improving drainage, which was true in the technical sense and incomplete in every other.

He backed his car out slowly, the reverse beep a small indignity in the quiet of the morning and parked it on the strip of higher ground at the far end of the cul-de-sac where the road had been built up slightly above flood grade. He had noticed this elevation the first time he drove down the street, twenty-three years ago, before they made an offer on the house. It was an eight-inch rise, barely perceptible. He had noted it in the way he noted all such things: the tide gauge position, the drainage culvert sizes, the barrier island distance, the elevation certificate, which he had requested from the county surveyor before they put in their offer and which Gloria had found on his desk and thought was routine, because for him it was.

He sat in the parked car for a moment.

The street was quiet. The Hendersons' house had its blinds down, which was new; they had always left them open, Lou Henderson a man who liked to see the street.

The Parkers two doors down had a For Sale sign, salt-faded from its third or fourth season in the yard. The Okafor family's van was loaded in the driveway; their youngest, a boy of about twelve, moved boxes from the front door with his head down and his arms full, the particular purposefulness of a child who had been given a real job. Frank watched him for a moment.

Frank got out of the car and walked back.

* * *

Inside, the house smelled of wet concrete and coffee.

The water in the living room was holding at two and a half feet, which meant the peak had probably passed. It would recede over the next several hours, leaving the familiar residue: the gray-brown tideline on the baseboards, the particular smell of silted water that got into the wall insulation and remained there for weeks, the slow damage to the subflooring that accumulated across floods the way compound interest accumulated in reverse, invisible and relentless.

Gloria was in the kitchen, which was elevated six inches above the living room on a foundation Frank had specified to the original contractor, in 1998, for reasons he had described at the time as aesthetic. She was making coffee with the deliberate focus she brought to everything, each movement controlled and unhurried, as if the water in the next room were simply weather. She had been making coffee in this kitchen for twenty-three years. She had made it through two previous floods. She set out two mugs and Frank sat at the counter on a stool and watched her and felt the familiar complicated thing he felt watching her do ordinary tasks in extraordinary circumstances, which was something he could not name and had not tried to name for a very long time.

"Marcus got through to the insurance line," she said, without turning.

"And."

"They're reviewing the claim criteria." She said this without inflection.

"It'll be the same as last time."

"I know it will."

She poured the coffee and turned and set a mug in front of him and stood at the counter with her own. She looked at him for a moment in the way she had looked at him for forty years, which was directly and with the sense that she was looking at more than what was visible, and Frank held the look and said nothing.

"Deja thinks we should start talking about next steps," Gloria said.

"Deja's been thinking that for a while."

"So have I."

Frank turned his mug a quarter turn on the counter. A thing he did when he was organizing his thoughts, which Gloria knew and which he knew she knew.

"We're not ready to have that conversation," he said.

Gloria looked at him. Something moved behind her eyes; not disagreement exactly, more like the recording of a fact she intended to return to.

"All right," she said. And turned back to the counter.

The sound of water in the living room.

Frank drank his coffee.

* * *

He went back to the deck in the early afternoon, after the water had begun to recede.

The family had dispersed to various tasks: Deja coordinating with the water remediation company by phone, Marcus documenting damage for the insurance claim, Isaiah somewhere in the house or possibly gone in his car, the quality of his absence ambiguous, as it had been for some time now. Amara was at a friend's house, which was on higher ground; they had dropped her the night before when the forecast came in. The house was quieter than it had been in the morning, which was the wrong word for it. Not quieter. Emptier. The procedural noise had served a function.

Frank stood at the railing and looked at the lawn, which was mostly visible again, brown and flattened, the grass pressed down by the passing water in the direction of its movement, a record of where it had been. The street was still standing water, calf-deep, which would take the rest of the afternoon to drain. The Okafors' van was gone.

He thought about the pencil lines on the post.

He thought about the 2019 report.

He thought about neither of these things in the sense of thinking about them deliberately; he had not thought about either deliberately for years. They were simply present the way chronic conditions were present: not requiring attention but always there, structuring what was possible, making certain thoughts available and others not. He had been a FDRA regional director for eleven years. Before that a floodplain management specialist; before that a civil engineer; before that a student from a town in Georgia that flooded every spring, who had decided at seventeen that there was something that could be done about that. The wood of the railing was warm under his palm. Damp still, but warm beneath the damp. He was standing on his deck watching the flood his own report had predicted, and he was thinking about nothing in particular.

That was the accurate description, or the one he reached for most often. Whatever he was supposed to feel in this situation, standing on the deck of a house his own report had condemned while his family worked behind him, he did not feel it in the way he imagined it should be felt. What there was instead was something more like accompaniment: a fact moving alongside him through time, present the way a chronic thing was present, which was to say always and in a way that had ceased to feel like anything at all.

He looked at the Gulf.

The overcast had thinned and the water out past the barrier islands was a pale gray-blue, the color it took in November, and there were pelicans on the sandbar to the east, which there always were. He had watched those pelicans from this railing for twenty-three years. They did not know about the report. They had no opinion about the rate of barrier island degradation, or the median projections in the appendix. They were pelicans, doing what pelicans did, and Frank watched them with the particular attention of a man who had learned to find rest in things that did not require him to know anything at all.

Behind him, inside, Deja was on the phone again.

He could hear her voice but not the words. The operational register: flat, efficient, solving something. She would be on the phone for another two hours at least, documenting and coordinating and managing the aftermath of a flood that was not the first and would not be the last. She had his mind for problems, Deja. She had his way with systems. He had watched her grow into a structural engineer with a pride that had nothing to do with her following him into a related field; he had not influenced that, as far as he knew. She had arrived there on her own.

He pressed his palm flat against the railing.

The wood was warm from the afternoon sun. Damp still, but warm beneath the damp.

He was seventy-one years old, and the house was standing and his family was in it, and the water was going back where it came from. These facts were also true. He held them alongside the other facts the way he had learned to hold them, which was not by resolving the contradiction but by finding a position from which the contradiction was simply the condition of things, the way a man who has lived long enough with a particular injury learns to stand so that it doesn't pull.

Deja came to the door.

He heard it slide open. He did not turn.

She stood there for a moment; he could feel her looking at him with the structural assessment her profession had given her, reading the load-bearing thing.

Then she went back inside.

He stayed.

The pelicans were still on the sandbar. One of them opened its wings briefly, for no apparent reason, and folded them again.

The water continued its unhurried retreat.

Frank stood at the railing and watched it go.

CHAPTER TWO:

Washington D.C. · 2019

He had prepared the presentation four times.

The first version ran forty-seven slides and took thirty-eight minutes to deliver at the pace he considered appropriate for material of this complexity. His deputy, a careful woman named Carla who had been with the agency longer than Frank and knew its appetite for information, suggested he cut it to twenty-two slides. He cut it to twenty-nine. She looked at him with the expression she reserved for situations she had decided not to argue about and said nothing further.

The morning of the presentation he woke at five-fifteen in the Marriott on L Street and lay in the distinct darkness of a hotel room where the blackout curtains were doing their job. He had not slept well. This was not unusual before significant presentations; he had given significant presentations for thirty years and had not slept well before most of them and considered this a reasonable tax on doing work that mattered. He lay in the dark and went through the report in the order he had arranged it, which was not the order the sections appeared on the page but the order in which he had determined the argument needed to land: the methodology first, because the methodology was unimpeachable and he wanted them to understand that before they understood anything else; then the baseline conditions, then the projection ranges, then the confidence intervals, then the implications for residential and commercial infrastructure, then the policy recommendations, which were modest and targeted and which he had drafted with the assistance of three colleagues whose judgment he trusted.

He had spent seven months on this report. The data collection had begun in early 2018; the modeling had taken four months; the drafting had taken six weeks; the internal review had taken another month, during which two colleagues had raised methodological questions he had considered seriously and answered in footnotes. The final document ran to two hundred and twelve pages, including appendices.

He was fifty-nine years old. He had been doing this work for thirty years. He knew what a good report looked like and this was a good report. That was not the same thing as knowing what would happen to it.

* * *

The Federal Infrastructure and Security Department conference room was on the fourth floor of the Nebraska Avenue Complex, a set of buildings that had been a girls' school before the Second World War and a naval intelligence facility afterward, and that now housed, among other things, the offices responsible for deciding what the federal government would publicly say about the long-range infrastructure implications of climate-driven coastal change.

Frank had been in this room before. Not this specific room, but rooms of this type: long table, projection screen at one end, water glasses, the particular quality of federal air conditioning that was slightly too cold for the summer clothes people wore to be in a building where the air conditioning was too cold. There were seven people seated when he arrived, which was three fewer than the list he had been given. He noted the absences without remarking on them and set up his laptop at the presenter's end of the table.

The senior official, whose name was Hartwell, was a man of fifty-five with the careful posture of someone who had learned to hold himself very still in rooms where things were decided. Frank had met him once before, briefly, at an agency function three years ago. Hartwell had the specific quality that Frank associated with people whose primary professional skill was the management of information: he asked good questions. He asked them in a tone that suggested genuine curiosity and at a pace that suggested he was already several questions ahead.

Two other officials. A note-taker. Two people Frank did not recognize, one of whom had a legal pad and one of whom had nothing visible in front of her, which Frank noted as a data point.

"Dr. Alderman," Hartwell said. "We appreciate you coming up."

Frank thanked him and began.

* * *

He had been presenting for eleven minutes when he understood that the report was not going to be acted upon.

It was not one thing. It was several things arriving in a sequence that Frank, who had spent thirty years reading the specific semiotics of institutional response, assembled into a conclusion before he had consciously named it. The note-taker's pen had slowed. The woman with nothing in front of her had shifted in her chair to a position that was very slightly turned away from him, which was the position of someone waiting for something to be over. One of the two officials he did not recognize had glanced at Hartwell with the barely perceptible check of a person confirming an arrangement that was already in place.

Frank kept presenting. He had spent seven months on this report, and he was going to finish presenting it.

He moved through the methodology. He moved through the baseline conditions. He moved through the projection ranges, which showed that thirty-eight thousand residential properties in the study corridor faced chronic inundation within fifteen years under median conditions, and that this number rose to sixty-four thousand under the seventy-fifth-percentile scenario, which was not the worst case. He said this clearly. He said it without drama, because the numbers did not need drama; the numbers were their own argument.

Hartwell leaned forward slightly when Frank reached the confidence intervals.

"These projections," he said. "These are your worst-case scenarios?"

Frank looked at him.

"No," he said. "These are the median projections."

A beat. Around the table, the quality of a room absorbing information it had not expected to receive in quite this form.

"The worst-case scenarios," Frank said, "are in the appendix."

Hartwell nodded. He wrote something on his notepad. He looked up with the expression of a man about to ask a question he had already decided the answer to.

"And the confidence interval on the median projection?"

"High," Frank said.

Another nod. Another note.

The room's temperature did not change. That was the tell. Frank had presented findings in rooms where the temperature changed: where someone leaned forward, where a side conversation began, where the note-taker's pen accelerated. This room did not do any of those things. The room remained exactly as it had been when he arrived, which meant the people in it had already decided what they were going to do with what he was telling them, and what he was telling them was not going to alter that.

He had been in enough of these rooms to know the difference between an audience receiving information and an audience managing the receipt of it. He finished the presentation. He moved through the policy recommendations, which were modest: revised flood-zone mapping, updated disclosure requirements, a phased infrastructure review. He said them in the order he had drafted them and, in the tone, he had cultivated for thirty years, which was careful and unhurried and which he had learned early was the only tone that sometimes worked, because any other tone gave the room a reason to classify the presenter rather than the information.

When he finished, Hartwell thanked him and said they would take the findings under advisement.

Frank closed his laptop.

"Under advisement" was the phrase the system used when it had decided. Not when it was deciding; when it had already decided and required a form of words that preserved the appearance of consideration for the duration of the meeting and for any documentation that might be generated from it. Frank knew this phrase the way he knew the flood projection lines: not as an abstraction but as a specific instrument with a specific function. He had been told before that things would be taken under advisement. Several of those things had subsequently been buried, revised, reclassified, or simply allowed to age in a database somewhere until the circumstances that had made them urgent were no longer urgent in a way that required action.

He thanked Hartwell and the room. He collected his materials. He shook the hands that were offered.

None of this took very long.

* * *

Outside, the August heat came off the Nebraska Avenue pavement in the way D.C. heat came off pavement in August, which was relentless and wholly indifferent to the interior conditions of people walking through it.

Frank walked to his rental car without hurrying. The distance was about four hundred yards. He was aware, in a way he could not quite describe, of walking through the distance between the room he had just left and the rest of his life.

He had spent seven months on the report. He had spent, if he counted from the beginning of his career, thirty years building toward the capacity to produce a report like it: the methodological rigor, the institutional standing, the accumulated professional credibility that meant the numbers in the document were not someone's estimate or someone's concern but a forensic accounting of what was going to happen, peer-reviewed and footnoted and presented to the people whose job it was to act on exactly this kind of information.

He got in the car and sat for a moment with his hands on the wheel, not starting the engine.

The thing that he had spent thirty years doing had been to reduce uncertainty. That was the job, understood at its most fundamental level: to replace the vague dread of something-is-wrong with the specific knowledge of what was wrong and when and to what degree. Uncertainty was not the enemy of action; he had always believed that. Uncertainty was the excuse for inaction. You reduced uncertainty and you removed the excuse and then the action followed, because the action was simply what rational people did when they understood the situation clearly.

He had understood, in the room, watching Hartwell's pen and the woman's turned shoulder and the barely perceptible consultation that had passed between the two officials he did not know, that he had been wrong about this. Not wrong about the data. Wrong about what certainty did to institutions. Certainty, it turned out, was not a solvent. In the right conditions, certainty was something institutions needed to manage, the way they managed any other substance that was useful in controlled quantities and dangerous in excess.

He sat in the car for a few more minutes.

Then he started the engine and drove to the airport.

* * *

He had a three-hour wait for his flight. He sat in the Delta terminal with a coffee he did not want and his laptop open to the document that would, within six weeks, be reclassified as internal distribution only and removed from the agency's public-facing database. He did not know this yet, though he suspected it. What he knew was that the phrase "under advisement" had been applied to it, and that the specific people who had applied it had the authority to determine what advisement produced.

He thought about calling Gloria. He had not told her much about the presentation, only that it was happening; he had not wanted to build expectations for an outcome that might not come. He was not sure now whether this had been a reasonable precaution or the first small choice in a sequence that was going to be harder to reverse the further along it went.

He did not call her. He told himself this was because the terminal was loud and the conversation would be unsatisfying. This was true. It was not the whole truth.

What he was not ready to say was that the report was not going to become policy. That the thirty-eight thousand properties were going to remain in their flood zones without the revised mapping. That the disclosure requirements were not going to be updated. That the phased infrastructure review was going to be advised upon indefinitely. That the house on the Gulf Coast that he and Gloria had lived in for eleven years, and that their daughter visited with her husband at Easter and Thanksgiving, and that was the best thing he had done with the money he had earned in thirty years of federal service, was sitting in the path of something he had now described, with forensic precision, in a document that was going to be taken under advisement.

He was fifty-nine years old and he had spent thirty years doing what could be done.

He sat in the terminal and drank the coffee and did not call home.

**

CHAPTER THREE:

I-95 South · 2019

The flight south left at six-forty and arrived at eight-twelve, and Frank spent most of it with his eyes closed, not sleeping but performing the approximate posture of sleep, which he had learned to do in the way you learned most things in a long career: through repetition and the gradual understanding that the performance was sometimes sufficient.

He had a window seat. Somewhere over South Carolina he opened his eyes and looked out at the darkness below, which was interrupted at intervals by the specific patterns of coastal settlement: the orange grids of towns, the thin lines of roads, and then the black absence of the water, which had no lights and no grid and no interruption, which simply was what it was from horizon to horizon.

He closed his eyes again.

He was thinking about the sentence he had read aloud in the conference room. Not about the room's response to it; he had understood the room's response clearly enough. He was thinking about the sentence itself, which he had written at eleven o'clock on a Tuesday three weeks earlier, choosing the words with the specific care he brought to plain-language translation: the requirement that a sentence mean exactly one thing to a reader who had not spent thirty years inside the vocabulary of flood risk management. He had read the draft to Carla the following morning and she had said it was clear, and he had sent it to the external reviewers, and they had not flagged it, and he had put it in the executive summary in the position where a reader would encounter it before they knew whether they wanted to.

The sentence had done what it was designed to do. It had meant exactly one thing.

This had not mattered.

* * *

The rental car was a mid-size sedan that smelled of the specific pine-scented cleaning product that rental car companies used to suggest cleanliness without achieving it. Frank adjusted the seat and mirrors with the mechanical efficiency of a man who had rented many cars and knew the adjustments he required and pulled out of the airport garage into the August night.

The I-95 south of Jacksonville was his road. He had driven it more times than he could account for: in both directions, in both daylight and dark, in weather ranging from the specific benevolent mildness of the Florida winter to the saturated heaviness of August, which was what it was tonight. He knew this road the way he knew certain things about his own body: not as information but as familiarity, the knowledge that lived below the level of attention and operated without requiring it.

He drove.

The highway at this hour was lightly traveled: trucks moving freight, a few passenger cars spread across the lanes with the particular dispersal of traffic that had not yet organized itself into rush-hour density. The lights of other vehicles moved past and away. The road itself was what it always was at night from inside a moving car: the constant presentation of illuminated tarmac, the white lines arriving and receding, the dark on either side that was the specific dark of flat coastal land at night, which was different from the dark of inland and different again from the dark of elevation, and which Frank had come to associate with a particular quality of openness; the sense of being visible in all directions even in the absence of light.

He was not thinking about the road.

He was thinking, in the way he had been thinking since he left the building on Nebraska Avenue, in a mode that was not quite thought and not quite feeling but something between them; the specific cognitive weather of a man in the process of understanding something he would rather not understand. The room had decided. The report was under advisement. Thirty-eight thousand properties would remain in their flood zones. The disclosure requirements would not be updated. The work he had spent seven months producing had been received, thanked, and filed in the category of things that would be looped in with relevant offices and considered in the context of ongoing initiatives, which was the category in which things were placed when the decision had already been made and the only remaining task was the management of appearances.

He knew this. He had known it before he left the building. He had known it, if he was honest, before he had left for Washington; had known it in the way you knew things you were not yet willing to act on, as a condition of the background rather than a fact in the foreground.

The background had now become the foreground. That was the only thing that had changed.

* * *

His phone was on the passenger seat.

He had put it there when he got in the car, face up, which was not his usual habit; he usually put it in the cupholder, face down, because the notifications disturbed his concentration when he was driving. Tonight he had put it face up without thinking about why.

Gloria's name was on the screen. He had opened her contact at some point, at the airport or on the plane or in the rental car garage; he could not pinpoint when. He had opened it and not called and now the screen showed her name and number and the green button that would connect him, and the screen's light was the brightest thing in the car.

He could call her. He was fifty-nine years old and he had been married to her for twenty-eight years and there was nothing in the world he did more fluently than talk to Gloria; no conversation he had had more practice with, no voice he was more certain of hearing on the other end of the line. He knew what she would sound like when she answered. He knew the quality of her attention on the phone, which was slightly more concentrated than in person because she could not see his face and compensated by listening more carefully to everything else. He knew what she would ask and roughly in what order, and he knew what his answers would be, and he knew that the conversation would take between twelve and twenty minutes and that he would feel, at the end of it, that he had said the things that were true and had not yet said the thing that mattered.

He knew this because he had been having this conversation, in various forms, for eleven years. Eleven years of technically accurate reporting on the state of the house, the state of the coast, the state of the projections in the folder in his office, which he always described in general terms as within normal parameters, because they were within normal parameters if normal was defined as expected rather than acceptable, and he had been defining it that way for long enough that the definition had become a kind of grammar he no longer noticed himself using.

He watched the road.

He could call her now. He could say: the report was buried today. They took it under advisement, which means they are not going to act on it, which means the projections I told you were within normal parameters are going to become normal, which means the house we built on the Gulf Coast is going to flood; not catastrophically, not in the way of a hurricane, but incrementally, the way things flood when the water table rises and the drainage system can no longer manage the load and the first floor goes underwater every few years and then more often and then the question of repair becomes the question of whether repair is the correct category. I should have told you eleven years ago. I should have told you before we made the offer. I knew the general shape of it then and I did not say so, and now I know the specific shape of it, forensically, and I am calling you from a rental car on the I-95 to tell you.

He did not call her.

He did not call her not because he had decided not to but because the decision was still forming, still in the zone between available and closed, and he was driving, and the phone was on the seat, and the road was presenting itself in the headlights with the same neutrality it always presented, and he was fifty-nine years old and tired in a way that was not the tiredness of a single day but the tiredness of a particular kind of sustained attention that had been running for twelve years and had now arrived at a juncture that required either a significant expenditure of that attention or the choice not to expend it.

The phone screen dimmed.

He looked at it.

The screen went dark.

* * *

He saw himself in the rearview mirror at some point south of Daytona.

He was not looking for himself; he was checking the lane behind him, the routine surveillance of a driver who had logged enough highway miles to check mirrors the way he checked tide gauges, as a matter of course, without expecting to find anything but needing to know. His own face appeared in the mirror, and he looked at it for a moment longer than was strictly necessary.

He was not sure what he expected to find there. Something, perhaps, that would tell him what he was in the process of deciding; some visible evidence of the interior condition he had been driving through for the past two hours. Guilt was the word that occurred to him, the obvious word, the one that a simpler accounting of the situation would have produced. But the face in the mirror did not look guilty, or not guilty in the way he understood guilt: the agitation, the self-consciousness, the quality of looking away from things.

He was looking directly at the mirror. His face was entirely still.

What he looked like, he thought, was a man in the process of accommodating himself to something. Not accepting it; not yet, and possibly never, but accommodating, which was a different operation: the adjustment of interior architecture to make room for a new permanent feature. He had seen this expression before, on other people, in other contexts; in the faces of colleagues who had been in the rooms where things were decided and had come out having learned something about how decisions were made. It was not a defeated expression. It was not even a sad one. It was the expression of someone who had updated their model of how the world worked.

He looked back at the road.

The world worked the way it worked. He had known this for a long time in the abstract and had now been given an instance of it. The room on Nebraska Avenue was not exceptional; that was the thing he was accommodating. It was representative. The report had been good, and it had not mattered because the question of whether the report was good was not the question that determined what happened to it. He had been operating, for thirty years, on the assumption that quality was at least a significant variable. He was updating that assumption.

This was not nothing. This was, in fact, considerable. But it was not the thing he would need to tell Gloria.

The thing he would need to tell Gloria was different. Smaller in one sense, larger in another: the thing that the report had confirmed about the house they lived in, the street they lived on, the eleven years of technically accurate general-terms reporting he had been conducting from the kitchen table and the phone and the occasional letter to Deja about the property's long-term prospects. He would need to tell Gloria that the folder in his office was not administrative documentation. He would need to tell her that the drainage channel he had built in the garage on a Saturday while she was visiting her sister had not been an aesthetic improvement.

He did not look at the phone.

The road continued south.

The coast road in August at eight in the evening was still warm, the air coming off the Gulf carrying the particular salt-and-vegetation smell that he associated with coming home, which was not where he had grown up but had become, over eleven years, the smell of arriving somewhere he had chosen. He had chosen it, knowing what he knew. That was the thing he had not yet examined directly: that he had known, before they made the offer, before they hired the contractor, before he had driven the first nail into the deck framing on a Saturday morning with Deja watching from the lawn and Gloria bringing coffee out at intervals, that the projections for this stretch of coast were not favorable. He had known in the general way that anyone working in coastal flood risk management knew about the Florida Gulf: the subsidence rates, the sea level trajectory, the hurricane intensification patterns. He had not yet run the numbers for this street, not formally. He had done that later, once they were living there, because it was the kind of thing he did, and the numbers had confirmed what the general knowledge had suggested, and he had put the numbers in a folder in his home office and not discussed them with Gloria.

This was twelve years before the third flood.

He had always intended to discuss them at some point. He had been waiting for the right moment, which had not yet arrived, and which he had come to understand, in the way you understood things you were not looking at directly, might not arrive on its own.

He pulled into the driveway.

The house was lit. He could see Gloria through the kitchen window, at the counter, her back to him. The particular domestic image of a person in a kitchen at the end of an ordinary day: the light above the stove, the small television on the counter she watched while she cooked, her posture that was always very slightly more upright than necessary, a remnant of the years she had taught school and stood in front of rooms full of people and learned to occupy space with precision.

He sat in the car for a moment.

The engine ticked as it cooled.

He could go inside and tell her. He had not yet decided not to. The decision was still available; it would be available for another thirty seconds, perhaps, before the inertia of the evening took over and the opportunity became the kind of opportunity that was technically still present but was, in practice, closed.

He watched her through the window.

She was cutting something. Her movements were efficient and familiar and entirely unaware of being watched - that was the intimacy: the way another person moved when they were not performing anything for anyone.

He had been married to her for twenty-eight years. He had not told her about the folder in his office. He had not told her about the projections for their street or the sea level trajectory for this stretch of coast or the subsidence rate or the hurricane intensification data. He had not told her because every time he had come close to it, the warmth of the kitchen window, the upright posture, the efficient movements of a woman who had chosen to live here with him, had made the information feel like a violence he was not yet willing to commit.

He got out of the car.

He went inside.

He did not tell her.

* * *

Gloria had made the grouper after all, with rice and a salad she had put together from the garden, and they ate at the kitchen table and she asked about the presentation and he said it had gone well, which was true in the narrow sense that he had delivered it without incident, and she said she was glad, and they talked about Deja's new project and a documentary Gloria had watched the night before and whether they should redo the deck boards, which were beginning to show their age.

After dinner he washed up and she dried. This was their arrangement. They did not talk while they did it, not because there was nothing to say but because this was one of the silences they had built together over twenty-eight years: the companionable silence of two people in a shared task, which was a different silence from the silence of concealment, and which Frank was careful to keep separate in his mind, because in his mind they were beginning to be adjacent.

That night he lay awake for a long time after Gloria had gone to sleep.

He was fifty-nine years old. The report was under advisement. The house was warm and specific and real around him; he could hear the Gulf from the bedroom window if the wind was right, which it was tonight, a low persistent sound that had become part of his sleep over eleven years, present the way chronic sounds were present, which was to say always and finally unheard.

He was not going to tell her.

He had not decided this. That was what he told himself, lying in the dark while the Gulf moved outside the window. He had not decided; he was simply not yet certain of the right moment, the right context, the right form of words that would allow him to say: the house we built together sits in the path of something I have spent thirty years measuring. He would find the right moment. It would come.

He lay in the dark and listened to the water and waited for the moment to arrive.

It did not arrive that night.

It did not arrive the following year, or the year after that. The report was reclassified. The disclosure requirements were not updated. The Coral Bay properties remained in their flood zones. The first flood came in 2024, in August, and the family executed the procedure that Deja and Marcus had put together from a template she had found online, and the water receded, and the house stood, and Frank repaired the damage to the subflooring himself on a Saturday over two weekends, and they did not discuss it in the way he had not discussed the folder in his office.

He was waiting for the right moment.

He understood, by the time of the second flood, that the right moment was a story he was telling himself. Not a lie, exactly; a structure. The kind of structure you built when the thing you needed to say had been unsaid long enough that saying it had acquired the weight of an event, and the weight of the event had become a reason to defer it, and the deferral had become its own accommodation.

He had spent thirty years reducing uncertainty. He had spent twelve years maintaining, in the house where he lived, a specific and very precise uncertainty in a person who trusted him.

He did not examine this directly. He had found that it was possible not to, if you were diligent about the other things: the subflooring repairs, the deck board assessments, the pencil lines on the post that recorded each flood's height, the tide gauge checks each evening before bed. If you were attentive enough to the management of the thing, you did not need to look at what you were managing.

This was, he recognized, exactly what the room in Washington had done with his report.

He recognized it. He did not say so. Not to Gloria. Not to Deja. Not to himself, in terms explicit enough to require a response.

He watched the water. He checked the gauge. He measured the lines on the post.

The water kept coming.

CHAPTER FOUR:

Highway 1 Motor Inn · 2031

Gloria had been asleep for two hours.

Frank could tell from her breathing, which had shifted sometime around midnight from the particular quality of someone performing sleep to the different quality of someone actually in it: slower, less attended, the specific loosening of a person who had given up the effort of consciousness. He had been married to her for forty years and he knew this shift the way he knew the tide gauge readings, as information that arrived through a sense he could not entirely account for but had come to trust.

He lay on the far bed and looked at the ceiling and listened to the air conditioning, which was producing a sound at the lower register of what hotel air conditioning typically produced, a sound that was less a cooling sound than a reminding sound: you are not at home, you are not at home, you are not at home.

He knew this. He had been not-at-home before. He had stayed in hotel rooms for thirty years of federal service, in cities whose names had become interchangeable after a certain number of years: the rooms were the same room, the ceilings were the same ceiling, the air conditioning was the same sound. He had learned to sleep in them, eventually, through the same mechanism by which he had learned most useful things: repetition and the gradual blunting of resistance.

Tonight he could not sleep.

He was thinking about the house.

* * *

They had driven down from Tallahassee on a Saturday in March, which was the best month to see the Gulf Coast: the winter visitors not yet gone, the summer humidity not yet arrived, the light at a particular angle that made the water do the thing the water did in March on the Florida Gulf, which was to be a color that did not correspond to any standard color description and that Frank had eventually stopped trying to name.

The realtor had shown them three houses. The first two were acceptable: the right square footage, the right school district, the right distance from the water. Frank had inspected them with the specific attention of a man who understood, professionally, what proximity to the Gulf Coast meant for a structure over time, and had found them adequate and said so, and Gloria had said they were fine, and they had eaten lunch at a seafood place on the waterfront and driven to the third house with the low expectation of a third house after two adequate ones.

The third house was on a street that curved gently away from the main road and ended in a cul-de-sac above a private inlet. The lot was larger than the others, the setback from the water more generous, the elevation higher by a measurement that Frank had noted on the listing sheet and that Gloria had not; she had been looking at the light. The light in the living room was coming through a set of west-facing windows that had been positioned, either by design or accident, at an angle that caught the afternoon Gulf light and distributed it across the interior in a way that made the room look like a room that had been lived in and loved for a very long time, though the house was eight years old.

"Oh," Gloria had said.

She had said it the way she said things she was not performing; quietly, to herself, to the room. Frank had looked at her looking at the light and had felt something he would not have known how to describe at the time, though he would have more opportunity in subsequent years to find the language for it: the quality of watching someone you love arrive somewhere they belong.

They made an offer the following week.

He had run the numbers before they signed. The elevation certificate was adequate; the FDRA flood zone designation was AE, which was the designation for areas with a one-percent annual chance of flooding, which was the designation that allowed reasonable people to proceed with reasonable caution and which Frank, at forty-eight, with thirty years of flood risk management behind him, understood to mean more than reasonable caution typically implied. He had also run projections, informal ones, using the data available at the time, and the projections had suggested a median timeline of twenty to thirty years before the property would face chronic inundation issues under conditions that were, at the time, considered median.

Twenty to thirty years was a long time. It was also not forever.

He signed.

* * *

The deck was his.

He had designed it himself, drawn it on graph paper at the kitchen table on a series of evenings in their first winter in the house while Gloria was at school board meetings, and had built it himself over the following spring with the help of a contractor friend named Delroy who had the skills Frank lacked and who worked on Saturdays for a rate that was below market and that Frank supplemented with a long-standing arrangement involving a trailer and several weekends helping Delroy move the accumulated inventory of Delroy's mother's house in Pensacola after she moved to assisted living.

He had built it to last. This was not a principle he articulated; it was simply the way he built things, the way his father had built things, the way of men from a certain generation and a certain part of Georgia for whom structures were either built to last or not worth building. He had chosen pressure-treated lumber at the specification above what the code required. He had used stainless steel fasteners when galvanized would have been sufficient. He had set the posts in concrete at a depth that accounted for frost heave, which was not a factor in Coral Bay but which was how he had been taught to set posts and which he had never seen a reason to stop doing.

Deja had been twenty. She had come out to the backyard on a Saturday in April and watched him work with the particular attention she had always brought to physical problems: assessing the structure, following the sequence, asking a question once and not again. He had put her to work handing him bolts, which she did without comment. They did not talk very much. He remembered the quality of that silence as one of the good silences, the kind that did not need to be filled because the activity was filling it.

When the deck was finished, Gloria had come outside with a bottle of wine and three glasses and Deja had been allowed a small amount mixed with a larger amount of sparkling water, which she had taken with the dignity of someone who had been included in something adult and understood the requirement not to make a fuss about it. They had sat on the new deck and looked at the water and Frank had felt the specific satisfaction of a thing built well: the solid feel of the boards underfoot, the plumb of the railing, the knowledge of what was holding it up and how long it would hold.

Twenty-three years later, the deck was still standing. The boards had been replaced twice; the railing once. The posts were the original posts. He had put them in correctly and they had stayed.

* * *

Deja had grown up in the previous house, in Tallahassee, and had arrived in Coral Bay at twenty, a young woman already beginning to read spaces the way engineers read them: for structure, for load, for what was holding things up.

She had taken to the water immediately. Not to swimming in it, though she could swim; to the fact of it, the way it was always there, always different, always requiring a different reading. She had inherited this from him, or he had cultivated it in her without knowing he was doing so; he was never entirely certain which. She would come to find him on the deck in the evenings and stand beside him and look at the Gulf with the focused quality she brought to things she was trying to understand, and sometimes she asked questions and sometimes she didn't, and he answered the questions he could and let the ones he couldn't stand.

She had asked him once, when she was fourteen, how you could tell how high the water was going to come.

He had told her about the tide gauges, the storm surge models, the relationship between barometric pressure and water height, the way the shape of the coastline affected surge amplification. He had told her about the barrier islands and what they were doing and how long they had been doing it and what the projections suggested about how long they would continue. He had told her this not as a lesson but as information she had asked for, in the way he answered all questions she asked him: directly, without simplification, trusting that she could absorb what was useful and let the rest wait until it became relevant.

She had listened to all of it.

"So we know it's going to flood," she said, when he had finished.

"Eventually," he said. "The question is the timeline."

"And what's the timeline?"

He had looked at the water.

"Long enough," he said.

She had accepted this. She was fourteen; long enough was long enough. She had gone back inside. He had stayed on the deck and watched the water and not examined, with any precision, what long enough meant or to whom it was sufficient.

She was forty-three now. She had become a structural engineer. He had not steered her toward it; she had found her way there herself, through an aptitude for the physical logic of things and a temperament that required her to understand, before she could proceed, what was holding something up. He watched her, sometimes, assess a building or a wall or a foundation with the specific focused attention she had once brought to the Gulf, and he understood that whatever she was doing she had learned, in part, from standing next to him on the deck and looking at something neither of them entirely understood yet.

He had given her that.

He had also given her the house she was currently trying to save from a flood he had predicted.

He did not examine this conjunction directly. He had found, over the years, that there were things that were better approached from an angle.

* * *

Gloria had made it her own in the specific way Gloria made everything her own, which was gradually, without announcement, through the accumulation of small decisions that each seemed minor and whose cumulative effect was total.

The kitchen first. She had repainted it within a month of moving in, a yellow that was not quite the yellow that had been there before and that Frank had noticed the difference of without being able to specify it. She had put up a shelf above the window and filled it with the particular items that appeared on Gloria's shelves wherever she lived: a small ceramic bowl she had bought at a market in Georgia twenty years before they moved to Florida; a photograph of her mother; a glass bottle she had found on a beach on their honeymoon that contained, she claimed, Atlantic Ocean water and which Frank had long since stopped questioning. The shelf had been the first sign. After the shelf came the rest.

She had spent most of her career in schools, which meant she understood, at a functional level, how to make a space legible to the people who had to live and work in it. She understood proportion and light and the specific effect of a plant in a corner on the emotional atmosphere of a room. Frank's taste in interiors ran to the adequate; he required that a space function and did not have strong opinions about what it looked like while functioning. Gloria had strong opinions, and had deployed them across twenty-three years of the house until the house was so completely hers that it was impossible to enter any room without feeling, immediately, that this was a room someone had thought about.

He had watched her do this the way he watched her do most things: with the admiring attention of a man who had found, early in the marriage, that he was not good at expressing admiration verbally and had compensated by paying very close attention to the things he admired, as if attentiveness were a language equivalent to speech. He did not know if she had understood this. He had never asked.

She had made the house beautiful. He had built the deck and repaired the subflooring and managed the drainage and run the numbers and she had made it beautiful, and the combination of these two kinds of care had produced something that was more than the sum of its parts; something that had the distinct character of a place that had been continuously and attentively inhabited, that held in its walls and its light and its proportions the record of everyone who had lived there and what they had done there.

He thought about the living room, the afternoon light coming through the west windows the way it had come through on the day they first saw it. The light had not changed. The windows were the same windows, the angle the same angle, the Gulf the same Gulf. What had changed was everything else: the furniture acquired and replaced, the walls repainted twice, the photographs that appeared on them and multiplied over twenty-three years until the walls held the record of a life that had been lived in the rooms below them. Deja as a child. Deja at her graduation. Isaiah at various ages, each one slightly harder to read than the last, until the most recent one, the year before last, in which he stood in the backyard looking at the camera with an expression that was neither hostile nor warm but simply private, the look of someone who had decided that the recording of their face was a transaction they could observe without fully participating in.

Isaiah had grown up in this house too, summers and Christmases and the occasional school holiday when Deja and Marcus needed coverage for reasons that were never entirely specified but that Frank and Gloria understood to mean: we need a break, and we trust you with him. Frank had watched him grow from the infant on his chest on the deck in 2024 to the fifteen-year-old who moved the car with the boredom of someone who had done it before. He was, of the people in the house, the one Frank understood least and watched most. There was something in Isaiah that Frank recognized without being able to name: a quality of attention directed outward, toward the world rather than toward the people immediately present, the quality of a person who was making calculations their family could not see.

Frank knew this quality. He had lived inside it for fifty years.

* * *

The thing he had not been prepared for, about the flooding, was the smell.

Not the smell of the water itself; he had anticipated that, had read the remediation literature, had understood what happened to insulation and subflooring and the underside of walls when water sat in them for more than forty-eight hours. He had understood it technically. What he had not been prepared for was the way the smell changed the house while the smell was in it; the way it displaced the smell that was normally there, which he had not known was a smell until it was absent.

A house had a smell. He had not known this, or not known it as knowledge he could use, until the first flood. The smell of their house had its own blend: Gloria's coffee, which she made in the same pot for twenty-three years and which left a signature residue in the air of the kitchen that was present even when no coffee was being made; the salt air that came through the windows when they were open and that had been coming through since they moved in; something underneath those things that was harder to name, the smell of the particular accumulation of a particular set of lives being lived in particular rooms over a particular stretch of time. He did not have a word for it. He had smelled it without knowing he was smelling it for twenty-three years.

The flood smell replaced it. Sat in the house for weeks afterward, diminishing slowly but never entirely gone until the remediation was complete. He had done the remediation himself after the first flood, replacing the baseboards and the lower sections of drywall and the subflooring in the two rooms that had taken the most water, and when it was done the house had been clean but not quite right for several months; had smelled of new materials rather than the accumulation that was the actual smell of the house, and he had waited, without discussing it with Gloria, for the accumulation to return.

It had returned. It always returned. This was something he had not expected: the resilience of a smell, the way a place reasserted itself after being violated by water, the way the character of a house that had been inhabited and loved reclaimed the air of its rooms as the materials dried and the lives resumed. He had been relieved by this each time in a way that was disproportionate to the thing itself, a relief that he understood, when he examined it, was not really about the smell.

He lay in the hotel room and listened to the air conditioning and thought about the smell of the house and waited for the morning.

* * *

The house was not a house.

He understood this clearly, lying in the dark while Gloria breathed her sleeping breath beside him. It was what houses became when people lived in them long enough and well enough: something that was also an account of the people who had built it and occupied it and repaired it and argued in it and cooked in it and sat on its deck in the evenings watching the water. It was the record of Deja handing him bolts on a Saturday in April. It was Gloria's shelf above the kitchen window, the ceramic bowl, the photograph of her mother. It was Isaiah at twelve running across the lawn, and at fifteen moving the car, and at two asleep on his chest in the early morning with the Gulf perfectly still behind them.

It was the proof.

That was the word he had been circling without landing on. The house was the proof of something; of a life assembled with care and inhabited with intention, of choices made that had produced this particular accumulation of rooms and light and smell and history. You did not leave the proof. To leave the proof was to admit that the thing it proved had been wrong, and he had spent thirty years building the thing it proved, and he had been fifty-nine years old on the afternoon he sat in a conference room in Washington and been told, in the polite and terminal language of institutions, that the thing he had spent thirty years building was not going to be sufficient.

He could not also leave the house.

Not yet. Not without the right moment. Not without finding the form of words that would allow him to say to Gloria: I knew, and I stayed because I could not bring myself to leave, and I stayed because leaving would have meant admitting that the thing we built together was built in the path of something I had been measuring for years and had not told you about. He could not say this without also saying: I chose the house over the truth. He could not say that without also saying: I chose it because it was the proof of everything I have done right, and I could not bear to stand in front of you and admit that the proof was standing in water.

He lay in the hotel room and looked at the ceiling and did not sleep.

Outside, somewhere below the window, a car moved through the parking lot and its headlights swept across the curtain and were gone.

Gloria breathed.

The air conditioning continued its low, patient reminder.

Frank closed his eyes and waited for the morning to come.

CHAPTER FIVE:

Coral Bay, Florida · 2031

Gloria had been reading Frank for forty years.

Not reading him the way you read a document, looking for the meaning behind the words. Reading him the way you read weather: registering pressure changes, the light, the way certain silences had a different texture from other silences and could be distinguished by someone who had been paying attention long enough. She did not do this consciously. She had stopped doing it consciously sometime in the first decade of the marriage, when the attention had become structural; part of the architecture of how she moved through a day.

She knew, for instance, that Frank was quieter after conferences in Washington than after field deployments. She knew that he slept worse in spring, which was when the tide data arrived for the fiscal year, though she could not have told you how she knew this since he had never said so. She knew his attention when he was working through something he had not named yet; a slightly increased attentiveness to the immediate and practical, an unusual care with small tasks, the way he would straighten things that did not need straightening.

She noticed these things without recording them. They were simply part of the information the day provided, like the temperature and the sound of the Gulf and whether the mail had come.

He had come home from Washington on a Tuesday in August, twelve years ago. She had read him in the driveway before he had crossed the threshold.

Something had changed.

She had not asked what.

* * *

She had been cutting an apple when he came through the door.

It was a thing she did sometimes in the evenings, a habit from the years when Deja was young and needed something in her hands while she did homework; the cutting of fruit into pieces on the board, the domestic rhythm of it, which required enough attention to keep the hands occupied and not enough to prevent thought. Frank had been in Washington for two days. She had been at school board meetings for most of them and had not had occasion to be quiet until now.

She heard him in the hallway: his keys on the hook, the particular sound of a man setting down what he was carrying. Then his footsteps to the kitchen doorway, where he stopped.

She finished the cut she was making before she turned.

This was not calculation. It was simply the way she managed the moment of reading: she needed a beat in which he was present and she was still, so that she could register the full information of him before the conversation started and the information became harder to separate from the words.

She turned.

He was standing in the doorway with the quality of a man who has been sitting in airports and airplanes for several hours and has arrived somewhere he was trying to get to and is not quite certain, now that he is here, that he knows what to do next. He looked tired. He looked, under the tired, like someone who had been reorganizing something interior and had not finished.

She read all of this in the time it took her to complete the turn.

"How did it go?" she said.

She watched him decide what to give her. It was a very small decision and it happened very quickly and she would not have been able to describe it to someone who had not spent forty years watching Frank make decisions. But she saw it: the slight adjustment in the set of his face, the choosing of the available rather than the true.

"Well enough," he said. "They're going to review it."

"That's good," she said.

She turned back to the cutting board. She picked up the apple.

There was a question forming in her that she was not going to ask. This was not suppression; she was not holding something down. She was simply deciding, in the way she decided such things, that the question was not one the evening could absorb. Not because the evening was fragile; she had forty years of evidence that evenings were less fragile than most people believed. But because the question, if she asked it, would require an answer, and she was not certain she wanted the answer in the form it would take on a Tuesday night in August when Frank had just walked through the door carrying whatever he was carrying, and the apple was half-cut, and the small television on the counter was doing the thing it always did, which was to be present without demanding anything.

She offered him an easier sentence instead.

"You're tired," she said.

It was not a question. It was a perimeter she was drawing: here is what this evening can hold. She watched him understand the drawing of it, and take what she had offered, and say yes, he was tired, and come to stand beside her at the counter with the familiar proximity of a man in his own kitchen after two days away.

She was aware that something had happened in Washington that he was not going to tell her tonight.

She finished cutting the apple.

She put it in a bowl and handed it to him and he took a piece and ate it and they were, for the moment, in the kitchen they had been in together for eleven years, and the Gulf was audible through the open window, and the small television murmured on the counter, and whatever had happened in Washington was somewhere to the left of the evening, held there by the discipline of a woman who had decided, without deciding, how much reality the evening could hold.

* * *

She had been a principal for eighteen years.

Before that, a teacher for nine. Twenty-seven years of reading rooms: the intelligence of a woman who had spent her professional life in buildings full of people who were, for various reasons, not saying the thing that mattered. Children did not say the thing that mattered because they lacked the language or the courage or the understanding that the thing could be said. Parents did not say it because they were performing competence, or protection, or the kind of denial that was not dishonesty but a form of hope. Staff did not say it because institutions rewarded the appearance of function over the substance of it.

She had learned, across those twenty-seven years, to read around the thing that was not being said. Not to excavate it; she had colleagues who excavated, who made it their business to find the unsaid and bring it into the light, and she had watched this approach produce as much damage as it resolved. She had learned instead to read the shape of the absence. To understand what the unsaid was by the negative space it occupied: what people avoided, what they circled, what they were elaborately careful about.

Frank was elaborately careful about the house.

This had been true for twelve years, and she had been reading it for twelve years, in the way she read such things: as information about the weather, not as evidence for a case she was building. She was not building a case. She was simply aware, with the awareness that came from forty years of paying attention to one person, that the house occupied a particular position in Frank's interior landscape that was not quite the position it occupied in hers.

He loved the house. She did not doubt this. But the quality of his love for it had a particular texture that her love did not have: something watchful in it, something that required him to be attentive to the house in a way that was slightly in excess of what the house, as a structure and a home, seemed to require. He checked things. He recorded things. He had built the drainage channel in the garage on a Saturday while she was in Tallahassee, and when she had asked about it on her return he had said he was improving drainage, and she had accepted this, and she had noticed, without making use of the noticing, that he had chosen to do it while she was away.

She had also noticed the folder in the second drawer of his desk, which she had seen once, briefly, when she had gone into his office to use the stapler. She had registered the label and not looked further, because his office was his office and she had always respected this, and because the label had been technical and he had a great many technical documents and this did not require explanation.

She had not forgotten it.

She did not know what it contained. She was not certain she needed to know what it contained. She was certain that it was connected to the particular quality of his attention to the house, to the drainage channel, to the tide gauge readings he checked each evening before bed, and to whatever had happened in Washington on that Tuesday in August.

These things cohered. She did not yet know into what.

* * *

The third flood was different from the first two, though she could not have said immediately how.

The procedure was the same. They had refined it after the second flood, Deja writing it up on her laptop at the kitchen table the following weekend while Frank looked at the drainage diagrams, and it had become the document that lived inside the cabinet above the refrigerator and that they had all read often enough not to need to read it anymore. The procedure ran. It had run well this morning. Everyone had known their role.

What was different was Frank.

He had stood on the deck while the family worked inside. She had seen him through the kitchen window: his back to the house, his hand on the railing, the particular posture that she had come to associate with him at the water, which was a posture of complete stillness that was different from rest because it was not restful. He watched the water the way she had seen him watch certain things over forty years: with the focused attention of someone who was reading information that was not available to casual observation.

She had seen this posture before the first flood, and before the second. She had seen it on evenings when the tide reports came in, and on the morning after storms, and occasionally on ordinary days for no reason she could identify. She had read it each time as the posture of a man who knew something about the water that she did not know, and she had not pressed him on it, partly because she trusted him and partly because she had decided, in the way she decided these things, that there were forms of knowledge that a marriage could hold in parallel without requiring them to be reconciled.

The third flood was the first time she had looked at the posture and felt, not curiosity, but the quality of a question she had been not-asking for a long time arriving at a threshold.

She did not ask it.

She went back to the cabinet.

She took down the bin with the photographs and carried them to the dining table and began the procedure of moving them to higher ground, one by one, handling each one with the care she had always brought to them: the care of a person who understood that photographs were not the events they depicted but were something else, the surviving record of the thing that had been, and that their survival mattered in a way that was not sentimental but was closer to a form of testimony.

She had saved photographs through three floods now. She was becoming an expert in the things that needed saving.

* * *

She placed her shoes neatly beside the bed.

This was a reflex, not a decision; the forty years of a tidy house, the habit of order that had survived displacement because it did not belong to the house but to her. She sat on the edge of the bed and looked at the photographs in the plastic bin by the door. She had not opened it since they arrived. She did not need to; she knew what was in it, had packed it herself, could have told you the order they were in.

Frank was at the window.

She read him from the back: the set of his shoulders, the particular quality of his stillness, which was not the stillness of rest but the stillness of sustained attention directed outward. He was doing what he always did at windows, which was to read what was in front of him. She had watched him do this in hotel rooms across thirty years of travel: the attentiveness of a man for whom the world was primarily information.

She looked at her hands.

She had been thinking, in the odd broken way that thinking happened in hotel rooms after long days, about the quality of Frank's silences over the past twelve years. Not any particular silence; the cumulative texture of them. The way certain questions had produced answers that were precise and correct and somehow slightly displaced from what she had been asking. The way his attention to the house had a quality that she could only describe, to herself, as grief, though it was grief for something that had not yet happened, which was not quite the right word but was the closest one available.

She had a word for this now, after the third flood, that she had not had before.

The word was: he knew.

Not knew what, precisely. She did not have that. But the pattern of the past twelve years, read as she read things, through the negative space and the shape of the absence, produced this: a man who had known something for a long time and had been carrying it in the way you carried something you could not yet put down.

She did not know if she was right. She had no evidence, only the accumulated reading of forty years applied to the particular weather of the past six. Evidence was not how she operated. She operated on the intelligence of sustained attention, which was a different instrument and not always a reliable one, and she knew this.

She decided not to decide, tonight, what she knew.

"Frank."

He turned from the window and sat on the far bed, facing her but not quite.

She looked at his face. She had been looking at his face for forty years and she could read it, she thought, better than he could; she had the advantage of seeing it from the outside, which was always an advantage when reading a face.

What she read was: a man who was managing more than he was showing, and who was managing it with the discipline of someone who had been managing it for a long time.

She asked him about the adjuster. She asked about the children, whether Renee could keep them through the weekend. She asked whether he had eaten, because he had the particular look of someone who had not. These were not the questions she was asking. They were the questions the evening could hold, the lateral questions, the ones that kept the conversation in the register of the solvable while she decided how much of the unsolvable to bring into the room.

"Are we going back?" she said.

Not: to the house. Not: tomorrow. Not: when the water recedes.

She heard herself ask the full question and understood, as she asked it, that it had arrived earlier than she had planned, that the evening had not held it at the lateral register as long as she had intended.

Frank heard it. She watched him hear all of it.

"I don't know," he said.

She heard the sentence land and felt, without being able to name why, that it cost him something to say it. That the insufficiency was not evasion. That something genuine was in it, alongside whatever was being withheld. She filed this without examining it.

She looked at his face for a moment.

"There's something you're not telling me," she said.

It was an observation, not an accusation. She had not reached for accusation; it was not the instrument she used.

He met her eyes. He said he was tired.

She held his eyes for three seconds.

Something in her face closed: not in anger, not in defeat, but in the resolution of a woman who had decided what the night could hold and who was now, with a precision that looked like acceptance, executing that decision.

"Okay," she said.

She reached for the lamp.

She did not say goodnight. She did not need to; goodnight was a sentence for evenings that had been ordinary, and this one had not been ordinary, and she was not going to pretend it had been by using the ordinary sentence.

She turned off the lamp.

Half the room went dark.

* * *

She lay in the dark and listened to Frank not lying down.

She could hear him on the far bed: the quality of a person sitting still in the dark, which was different from the quality of a person lying in the dark because it was sustained in a way that lying was not, held upright by something that had not yet permitted him to let go of the vertical.

She did not speak to him.

She was thinking about the photographs in the bin by the door. Not any particular photograph; the fact of them. That she had packed them and carried them through three floods and that they were still here, that the record they contained had survived, that the faces they showed were still the faces of people who were alive and were in the world and were going to wake up tomorrow.

This was not a small thing.

She was also thinking about the question she had asked, and the way he had heard it, and the way the answer had been true and insufficient, and what the insufficiency contained. She was a woman who had spent twenty-seven years in rooms where the thing that mattered was not being said, and she knew the weight of it; knew the specific cost to the person not saying it, and the specific different cost to the person not receiving it. The costs were not the same. They were not even the same kind of thing.

She did not know what Frank was not telling her.

She knew it was there. She had known it was there for twelve years, in the way she knew weather: not as a fact that could be verified but as a condition that could be read. She had been deciding, each day of those twelve years, how much of that reading to act on; how many questions the marriage could absorb without requiring the answer she was not certain she was ready to have.

She had been protecting herself. She understood this now, in the dark of a hotel room that smelled of chlorine, with Frank sitting upright on the far bed and the Gulf somewhere outside the window doing what the Gulf did. She had been protecting herself from the answer by choosing which questions to ask, and she had been doing this not unconsciously but with the specific intelligence of a woman who knew what she was doing and had decided it was the right thing to do.

She was not certain anymore that it was.

This was not a decision. It was a shift in the weather: a change in pressure that preceded a change she could not yet name. She lay in the dark and felt it and did not speak.

On the far bed, Frank sat in the dark and did not lie down.

Between them, in the middle of the room, the thing he was not telling her occupied the space the way temperature occupied a room: invisible, total, registered by both of them without acknowledgement.

The air conditioning continued its patient work.

Gloria closed her eyes and waited for the morning.

CHAPTER SIX:

Coral Bay, Florida · 2031

The office was the driest room in the house.

Frank had designed it that way. When they were building out the interior in 1998, he had specified a raised threshold at the office door, a half-inch lip that most contractors would have questioned and that Delroy had installed without comment, understanding without being told that this was a room that was intended to remain separate from whatever the rest of the house experienced. The floor was hardwood over a concrete subfloor sealed with an epoxy he had applied himself the summer after the first flood, working on a Saturday in the particular focused way he worked on things that mattered, which was methodically and in silence.

He had been protecting the office for twelve years.

He understood now, standing on the deck and watching the water move across the lawn, that he had been protecting a folder as much as a room.

* * *

He heard her go in.

Not the door specifically; the door was at the back of the house, and he was on the deck. But he had been attuned to the sounds of the house for twelve years with the specific attentiveness of a man who was waiting for something, and he heard the change in the acoustic of the interior: a pause in the procedural sounds, a particular quality of stillness from the direction of the hallway, and then the creak of the office floor that he knew as well as any sound the house produced because he had walked across it every day for twenty-three years.

He did not move immediately.

He stood at the railing and watched the water and waited to see if the sounds resolved. They did not resolve. The stillness held. He heard, very faintly, the particular sound of a drawer.

He turned from the railing and went inside.

* * *

He walked down the hallway with the deliberate pace of a man who was not rushing because rushing would mean that he knew why he was going there, and he did not want to know yet, or did not want to have been right about what he knew.

The office door was ajar.

He could see, through the gap, the edge of the desk and Deja's shoulder and the particular quality of her attention, which he recognized because he had watched her pay that quality of attention to things for forty-three years: the complete focus, the slight forward lean, the stillness of the rest of her body while her eyes moved. She paid that attention to structures she was assessing; to problems she was solving; to things she was trying to understand.

He put his hand on the door.

He already knew.

He opened it.

* * *

She looked up.

A beat: the length of one breath in which neither of them moved. Frank standing in the doorway. Deja at the desk. The folder open between her wet hands. The map on the page she had stopped on, with its projection lines running inland from the Gulf in the colors he had chosen for the report because he had believed, at the time, that color coding would make the data more legible to people who did not read technical documents.

He had believed, at the time, in the power of legibility.

He entered.

He closed the door behind him, with the care he brought to doors in this house, which was the care of a man who had built the frames and knew their tolerances.

He crossed to the desk and sat beside her. Not opposite; beside. He did not put the desk between them. He was not certain why he made this choice except that it was the choice his body made before his mind had caught up, and he had learned to trust this kind of prior choice because it was usually the more honest one.

She looked at the folder. Then at him.

"What is this?" she said.

Her voice was level. She was asking as an engineer; he could hear it. The technical register, the request for classification. She had not yet arrived at the other question.

"A projection study," he said.

"For what."

His eyes moved to the title on the cover page, which he knew by heart.

"Coastal residential viability."

"Obsolescence," she said. She was reading the actual word on the page, which was the word he had used because it was the accurate word.

"That was the internal term," he said.

"Reclassified?"

"Yes."

"By who."

"Not me."

She looked at the page again. He watched her read it the way he had read it: following the methodology, assessing the data quality, checking the confidence intervals. She was a structural engineer. She understood load-bearing things. She was applying her professional intelligence to his document in the same way she would apply it to a building, and he watched the process with the terrible attention of a man watching something he has been dreading for twelve years begin to happen.

"These are worst case?" she said.

He looked at the map the way you looked at an old wound: knowing what you would find there, unable to look away.

"Median," he said.

"Confidence?"

"High."

She absorbed this. She turned a page. He watched her follow the street grid with her finger, the way she had followed countless plans across her career, reading the geometry of a place to understand what it could and could not bear. Her finger slowed. Found the street. Found the address. Found the outline of the lot.

Their lot.

Her hand stopped on the page.

She had been reading this as a technical document.

She was no longer reading it that way.

* * *

She looked at him.

The look was not the look of someone who had found something they were searching for. It was the look of someone who had found something they had not known they were searching for, and who was now reconstructing, at speed, a version of the past that accommodated this finding. He could see the reconstruction happening. He had watched Deja process information her whole life and he knew the quality of her face when the processing was producing a result she had not anticipated.

"You knew," she said.

Not a question. A calculation completed.

"Yes," he said.

"When."

"2019."

The number landed between them.

Twelve years. He watched her do the arithmetic without looking away from him. Twelve years from the report to the third flood. Twelve years of tide gauges and pencil lines and the drainage channel in the garage and the careful attention to a house he had privately condemned. Twelve years of her growing up, of Isaiah being born on this street, of Gloria's shelf above the kitchen window and the photographs on the walls and the particular smell of a place that had been inhabited and loved.

Her face changed. Not into anger; he had been braced for anger and it did not come. Into something that was, he thought, worse than anger: comprehension. The precise comprehension of an engineer who had just understood the load-bearing structure of something she had been living inside.

* * *

"Why didn't you-"

She stopped. She was too precise to finish a sentence she had not yet located the right words for. She tried again.

"Why didn't you tell us."

Frank looked at her.

The question was the question he had been not-answering for twelve years, asked now directly across the desk of the room where he had kept the document that made it answerable, and he was aware that the answer existed; it had existed for twelve years, in various forms, forming and dissolving in his interior the way a word formed and dissolved when you could not quite bring it to articulation. He had the answer. He had had it for twelve years. He had simply never found the form of words that would allow him to say it.

He opened his mouth.

The word was: because.

Because was easy. Because was the beginning of the sentence that could not begin.

He closed his mouth.

He looked at his hands on the desk. They were steady. This was, he understood, the problem. A man with shaking hands was a man whose distress was legible, was available to comfort, was convertible into the ordinary human exchange of one person steadying another. His hands were completely still. There was nothing in them for Deja to hold.

He looked back at her.

"Because then you would have...."

He stopped.

The sentence had arrived at the word that was the real word, the word behind because, and he could feel it there, available, requiring only the continuation of the sentence to become speech, and the sentence would not continue. Not from cowardice; he had crossed a threshold somewhere in the hallway, he thought, or perhaps in the conference room in Washington twelve years ago, or perhaps in the car on the I-95 with his phone on the passenger seat, where cowardice was no longer the operative category. From incapacity. From the incapacity of a man who had organized his interior life around a particular configuration of knowledge and concealment for so long that the alternative configuration was simply unavailable; he could not access it any more than he could access the version of himself who had walked into the conference room in Washington believing that legibility produced action.

"Because then you would have left."

Deja flinched. Almost imperceptibly. He saw it.

He looked down at his hands again.

"And I..."

The sentence stopped there. He could feel, in the remaining space of it, everything that it was trying to say: the years of early mornings with the tide gauge; the pleasure of the deck he had built; the weight of Amara on his chest on a perfect summer morning; Gloria's shelf above the kitchen window and the particular warmth of a lit kitchen at the end of a day; the proof of a life assembled with care and inhabited with intention; the knowledge that to leave the proof was to admit that the thing it proved had been built in the path of something he had been measuring for thirty years and had not told them about. All of it was in the remaining space of the sentence. He had no idea how to put any of it into the sentence. The sentence was two words and a gap.

He reached for the folder.

* * *

He closed it slowly.

The way you closed something that had weight: attending to it, not letting it fall. He slid it back into the drawer. He heard the click of the drawer closing. He sat with that sound for a moment.

Then he stood.

He turned toward the door and stopped.

He looked back at her.

She was sitting very still, her hands in her lap now, her face doing the thing it did when she was waiting: not the impatience of a person who wanted something to happen but the focused patience of a person who understood that the next development was not theirs to control.

He had one thing available. It was not the sentence. It was not the answer to the question she had asked. It was the thing he had always had: the practical, the immediate, the management of the next small need.

"Do you want coffee?" he said.

The words were entirely ordinary. In the context of the room they had just been in together, in the context of the folder he had just closed and the sentence he had not been able to finish, they were the most terrible thing he had said. He knew this as he said them. He said them anyway because they were the only thing he had.

Deja looked at him for a moment.

The look held everything she had just understood and everything she had not yet decided and everything that was going to be required of her in the weeks and months ahead. He had carried something for twelve years. He had just transferred part of it to her, without asking, without explaining, without finishing the sentence.

"Yeah," she said.

He nodded. He turned toward the door.

Behind him, Deja looked at the desk. She looked at the damp marks her hands had left on the surface: on his desk, on his report, on his twelve years of silence. She had been in this room for ten minutes and she had already left her mark on it.

She left them there.

She stood.

She followed him.

* * *

The kitchen was operating on two registers simultaneously.

On one register: the flood. The waterproof bin on the counter, the towel spread flat for a work surface, the particular sound of the water in the living room that was louder than it should have been through the kitchen wall, the procedural sounds of a house managing a third emergency. On the other register: what had just happened in the office, which had no sound at all and occupied the kitchen the way a temperature occupied a room: invisibly, totally.

Frank filled the kettle. He measured the coffee with the ritual precision he brought to this task in this kitchen; the ritual care of a man for whom the making of coffee was not a preference but a grammar, a way of organizing the immediate while the not-immediate remained in its unresolved state.

He set out two mugs. He did not ask which one she wanted. He already knew.

Deja sat at the table, diagonal to where he would sit. Not directly across; diagonal. A position that allowed them to be in the same room without requiring them to look at each other except by choice.

He poured. He set her mug in front of her. His hand stayed a half-second too long on the handle before he let it go.

She wrapped both hands around the mug. The warmth was real. That was the truth of it: entirely real.

He sat.

Outside the kitchen, the house continued. Marcus on the phone somewhere; the specific cadence of a man arguing with an institution, which Frank recognized. Isaiah's voice, briefly, saying he had moved something. Gloria somewhere, efficient and unhearable.

"Water's coming up faster than last time," Frank said.

It was true. It was also the available sentence; the lateral statement, the one that referred to the flood rather than the office.

"Mm," Deja said.

She sipped. The coffee was too hot. She did not react.

He watched her not react.

This, he thought, was what he had given her. Not the folder; not the twelve years or the reclassified report or the pencil lines on the deck post. This: the specific discipline of receiving information you cannot yet act on and continuing to function. He had modelled it for her entire life. She had absorbed it the way she absorbed everything he had given her; completely and without acknowledgement, until one day it was simply part of how she moved through the world.

He was not certain this had been a gift.

The kitchen door moved. Gloria, in transit: wet trousers, photographs in her arms, the particular efficiency of a woman executing a procedure she had refined across three floods. She slowed.

Her eyes moved: Frank's back. Deja's face. The space between them. Three seconds.

Something registered in her face that was not recognition of what, not yet; recognition that something had changed the quality of the air in the kitchen.

"I'm taking these to the hotel bag," she said.

She left.

Frank did not turn.

The kitchen held what it held.

Deja looked at her mug. Then at him.

"So you just tracked it," she said. "All this time."

"I didn't want you to carry it," he said.

She looked at him with the intent expression of someone who had been handed a sentence and was turning it over to examine its underside.

"But you did," she said.

He nodded.

Neither of them spoke for a moment. The house continued around them: the water in the living room, the insurance call, the particular sounds of three floods worth of competence being deployed in the rooms adjacent to the kitchen. The real disaster was sitting at the kitchen table with two mugs of coffee between it and ordinary life.

"I have to figure out what to do," Deja said.

He nodded again.

"Don't make me do it alone," she said.

Something moved in his face. Not relief; the situation did not admit relief. Something more like the distinct recognition of a person who has been carrying something alone for a very long time and has just been offered, obliquely, the possibility of not doing so.

"I'm here," he said.

The kitchen clock continued its work. The house groaned with the unmistakable sound of a structure accommodating a load it had been asked to bear before

Frank and Deja sat with their coffee and the thing between them that was not the coffee.

CHAPTER SEVEN:

Coral Bay, Florida · 2031

They went back on Thursday.

The water had receded by Wednesday morning, and the adjuster came Thursday afternoon and moved through the house with the specific efficiency of a person who had seen this before and was performing assessment rather than surprise. He had a clipboard and a camera, and he said the same things adjusters had said after the first flood and the second: chronic inundation damage, policy review required, timeline for response six to eight weeks. Frank listened to him the way he listened to things he already knew, which was attentively and without reaction. He thanked the adjuster at the door. He watched him drive away.

Then he went inside and looked at the waterline on the baseboards.

The line was three inches higher than the second flood. He knew this before he measured it. He had known, on the deck during the flood, reading the boards, what the high-water mark would be when the water pulled back. He measured it anyway, because measurement was what he did, and because the number needed to exist somewhere other than in his knowledge.

He wrote it in the notebook he kept in the second drawer of the desk.

He put the notebook away.

He did not look at the folder.

* * *

Deja and Marcus stayed through the weekend.

This was not unusual after a flood; there was always remediation work in the first days, and Deja managed it the way she managed everything: with a clipboard and a sequence and the focused competence of a structural engineer who had grown up watching her father manage crises and had inherited the method if not, apparently, all of the information that informed it. She was good at this. She had always been good at this. Frank watched her work and felt the thing he had been feeling since Thursday, which was the uncomfortable quality of watching someone demonstrate a capability you had given them and understanding, now, what it had cost.

They did not speak about the office.

Not avoidance, exactly; avoidance required an active decision to go around something, and they had not made that decision. They had simply not found the occasion. The house was full of the particular busyness of post-flood remediation: contractors, assessors, the insurance company's secondary reviewer, the concrete practical conversations that a house in this condition required. Frank and Deja moved through these conversations efficiently and in parallel and the subject of the office did not arise because the subject of the office was not a practical matter and the week was made entirely of practical matters.

This was not a coincidence. Frank understood that the week's practical density had a function beyond its practical content. He did not examine this understanding directly.

He watched Deja, across the week, the way he had always watched her: attentively, from a slight distance, reading the information her posture and her movements provided. What he read now was different from what he had read before Thursday. Before Thursday, he had read a daughter who was managing a flood with competence and controlled frustration. Now he read a daughter who was managing a flood and something else simultaneously, in the way he had managed something else simultaneously for twelve years: efficiently, without visible strain, with the particular quality of attention that came from being required to maintain two registers at once.

She had learned quickly.

He was not certain this was something to be proud of.

* * *

Marcus was at the kitchen table with the damage spreadsheet when she came in from the garage.

He had been methodical about it, the way he was methodical about everything: columns for location, damage type, estimated repair cost, prior occurrence. He was good at this. Deja had always been grateful for this in him, the way he moved through practical problems with the same unhurried precision she brought to structures, without her needing to ask.

He looked up when she came in.

"Subflooring in the living room," he said. "There's prior repair evidence - I can see where you patched after the second flood. Do I document the history or just current condition?"

She set the clipboard down on the counter.

"Current condition," she said. "Document what we can see now. Not the history."

A beat.

She heard it as she said it. The double weight of a sentence that meant exactly what it said and also something else entirely, something she had no intention of saying, something she was apparently not able to prevent from surfacing in the precise language she chose for ordinary things.

Marcus looked at her.

He had been married to her for sixteen years. He knew the register of her competence when it was covering something. He knew, and she knew he knew, and the knowing sat between them in the kitchen the way certain things sat: not requiring speech, not available for speech, simply present.

"Deja," he said.

She picked up the clipboard.

"Write it the way I said," she said. "Current condition only."

He wrote it the way she said.

She went back to the garage.

* * *

Gloria noticed.

She did not say what she noticed. She moved through the week with her usual efficiency, managing the parts of the remediation that required managing, cooking in the half-functional kitchen, talking to Renee about the children, doing the specific practical things that the week required. But Frank could feel, in the way he could always feel Gloria's attention, that her reading of the household had shifted register. She was paying a different attention to the rooms.

She was paying attention to the space between Frank and Deja.

He knew this because she had always paid attention to the space between people; it was what forty years of professional life in schools had given her, the distinct skill of reading the negative space in a room, the distance between bodies, the quality of silences that occurred in certain configurations and not others. He had watched her deploy this skill across their marriage with the appreciation of someone who recognized expertise he did not possess. He could not now be surprised that she was deploying it here.

She asked him, on Saturday evening, whether Deja seemed all right to him.

It was a lateral question. He recognized it as such. He had been living with Gloria's lateral questions for forty years and he knew their shape; the way they approached the actual question from an angle, addressing something adjacent rather than the thing itself.

"She's managing well," he said. "The remediation's on track."

Gloria looked at him for a moment.

"That's not what I asked," she said.

He met her eyes. He said Deja seemed fine to him; she had a lot on her plate, she always had a lot on her plate, she handled it the way she always did.

Gloria accepted this. She turned back to what she was doing.

He stood in the kitchen for a moment after she had turned, looking at her back, and felt the exact weight of a room that contained three people with different portions of a truth that none of them had all of.

* * *

He could not find the folder on Tuesday.

Not lost; he knew it was in the office. He had not moved it since the day Deja had found it, had not opened the drawer since he had clicked it shut, had not done anything that would have altered its location. But on Tuesday morning he opened the drawer to check something in a different file and found himself, before he had consciously decided to look, looking at the place where the folder should be.

It was not there.

He stood in the office for a moment with his hand on the drawer.

The first thing he felt, before he had identified what was happening, was something that took him a beat to name: relief. A physical release of something he had been holding, arriving before he had understood what he was holding or what its absence would mean. Relief at the absence of the folder.

This troubled him. He stood in the office and let it trouble him, which was an unusual experience; he generally did not let things trouble him in real time, had learned over the years to process disturbance at a distance. But the relief had arrived so quickly, so physically, and with such specificity, that he found himself attending to it before he could redirect his attention elsewhere.

He had spent twelve years protecting that folder. Keeping it in its drawer, sealed, in the second-from-bottom position where a casual search would not find it. He had protected it through two floods and a reclassification and Deja's discovery of it and the conversation that followed, and on a Tuesday morning in the week after the third flood his first response to its apparent absence had been relief.

He checked the drawer again. More carefully this time, moving the other files aside. The folder was there, pushed to the back by the movement of the drawer's contents during the flood, behind a thicker binder that had shifted forward and obscured it. It had not gone anywhere. It was exactly where it had been.

He put the binder back.

He closed the drawer.

He sat in his chair for a while and looked at the commendation plaque on the wall that nobody dusted anymore and did not think about what the relief had meant, because he was not ready to think about what the relief had meant, and thinking about things before you were ready to think about them was a habit he had learned, across thirty years of professional life, produced conclusions you were not yet equipped to use.

He would think about it later.

He went to find Gloria to ask about lunch.

* * *

The reclassification had come through in October of 2019.

Carla had called him on a Wednesday afternoon, her voice carrying the careful tone of someone delivering information they were required to deliver and would have preferred not to. He had thanked her. He had sat in his office and looked at the commendation plaque, which had still been relatively new at that point and which he had not yet developed the habit of not-looking-at that he would develop over the following years. Then he had driven home.

He had not told Gloria that evening either.

He had intended to. He had driven home intending to, in the way he had driven home from Washington intending to, with the sense that this was the evening when the circumstances would be right, when he would find the form of words, when the conversation would become available. He had come in through the door and she had been in the kitchen and he had stood in the doorway and looked at her, and the warmth of the kitchen in October and Gloria at the counter and the Gulf just audible through the window had produced the same thing it always produced, which was the understanding that saying it now would change the quality of this moment and all subsequent moments, and he was not ready for that change.

He had not been ready in November either.

Or in the spring, when the first serious tidal surge came and went without crossing the threshold into the house, and he had read the measurement on the gauge and marked his private accounting and told Gloria the Gulf was a little high this week. Or the following summer, when the projections he had been tracking suggested the first flood was two to four years out under median conditions, and he had built the drainage channel in the garage and told her he was improving drainage.

The first flood came in August 2024.

He had known two weeks in advance, from the tide data and the storm track, that it was coming. He had spent those two weeks doing the practical things: reinforcing the threshold seals, checking the waterproof containers, confirming the procedure with Deja, who had put together the protocol document without knowing why her father had been so specific about certain preparation details. He had spent those two weeks not saying: this is the first one. He had spent the first flood itself on the deck, watching the water come in, and had understood in his body what he had known in his data for five years, which was that this was not an emergency but a beginning.

He had repaired the subflooring himself over two Saturdays. He had marked the first pencil line on the deck post, low on the wood, where no one would think to look for it. He had told himself he was waiting for the right moment to tell Gloria.

He told himself this for seven more years.

The right moment was a moving target. It was always positioned just past the current moment, in a future where the circumstances were better and the words were clearer and the truth could be delivered in a form that did not also deliver everything that came with it: the eleven years of technically accurate incomplete reporting; the drainage channel on a Saturday; the garage, the tide gauge, the notebook in the second drawer; the careful management of her uncertainty that had been, all along, a management of his own inability to close the distance between what he knew and what he could say.

He had not found the moment.

He had found, instead, a third flood and a daughter who had found the folder and a kitchen table where two people now sat with their coffee in the familiar proximity of people who were carrying the same thing and had not yet decided what to do with it.

* * *

By Sunday the house had been returned to a version of itself.

Not the same version; the baseboards would need replacing, and the smell of the water would be in the walls for weeks, and the particular quality of the light in the living room was different in the way the light was always different for a period after a flood, as if the water left something in the air as it retreated. But the furniture was back in place, the photographs were back on the walls, the kitchen was functional, the procedure had been executed and the house had survived it.

Deja and Marcus left Sunday afternoon. The children were brought back from Renee's. Isaiah came through the door with the quality of a teenager returning to a place he had partly left already; present in body, attentive in a way that was not quite the attentiveness of someone invested in the place but the attentiveness of someone reading it, taking its current measurements. He moved through the rooms and said the right things and went upstairs.

Frank watched him go.

Gloria was in the kitchen. Frank could hear her putting things back in order, the small sounds of a woman restoring the exact arrangement of a space she had spent twenty-three years making into what it was. He stood in the hallway between the kitchen and the office and listened to those sounds and felt the weight of the week settling around him in the particular way weight settled when the busyness that had been keeping it distributed was no longer there to distribute it.

He thought about Deja's car leaving. The sight of it pulling out of the driveway with the practiced efficiency of someone who had been doing this for years: reversing, checking, going. She had not looked back. He had watched from the porch, and she had not looked back, and he had understood this as information but had not yet determined what it was information about.

He went into the office.

He sat at the desk.

He did not open the second drawer.

He sat for a while in the room that had been the center of something and was now, again, just a room: his books, his binders, the commendation plaque, the framed photograph of the house from years ago when it had been new and the light through the west windows had fallen on Gloria's face and she had said oh in the particular way that meant she had arrived somewhere she recognized.

The house was quiet.

From the kitchen, the small sounds of Gloria putting things back where they belonged.

Frank sat in the silence and let it be what it was.

CHAPTER EIGHT:

Coral Bay, Florida · Various

There was a question Gloria had not asked Frank for twelve years.

Not the same question every time. It was more like a country than a question; a territory she had been navigating around, approaching from different directions at different times, finding the edges of it without crossing in. The edges were recognizable by a particular quality of the air just before she reached them: a slight change in temperature, an adjustment in the quality of Frank's attention when her sentences moved in certain directions. Not as knowledge you could articulate. As a kind of proprioception.

She had not always been this careful.

In the first years after they moved to Coral Bay, she had asked him things directly. She had asked about the elevation certificate, which he had produced and explained with the professional fluency he brought to technical questions, and the explanation had been accurate, and she had understood it and they had bought the house. She had asked, in the second year, why he had specified a raised threshold for the office door, and he had said he preferred to keep the paper files dry, and she had accepted this because it was reasonable and because there was nothing in his face when he said it that suggested it was not the whole answer.

She had asked, in the third year, about the drainage channel.

She had come home from Tallahassee on a Sunday afternoon to find the garage floor newly excavated along its back wall, the concrete saw marks still sharp, a channel that had not existed that morning now running the full length of the back wall toward a drain he had apparently also installed. He was cleaning up when she arrived. She had asked what it was. He had said he was improving drainage. She had looked at the channel and then at him and had said: improving from what?

He had looked at her with the expression she had been learning to read: not evasion, not guilt, but something more careful than the expression of a man who simply improved drainage on a Saturday while his wife was out of town. A management.

She had taken it at face value.

She had decided to take it at face value. She was clear about this, in retrospect; it had not been naive or unconscious. She had looked at him and at the channel and she had made a choice: that the available explanation was sufficient for the moment, and that the insufficient-feeling explanation she suspected was behind it was not something she needed tonight.

She had not understood, then, what she was choosing.

* * *

She had developed, across the following years, a vocabulary for what she was doing.

Not words; she had not put words to it. A practice. The quiet practice of a woman who had spent twenty-seven years in schools reading the difference between what was being said and what was true, and who had brought that skill home and applied it to her marriage. Knowing when not to read.

She had become very good at knowing when not to read.

There were subjects that had a gravity in Frank's vicinity; subjects that, when approached, produced in him the management she had learned to identify. The house was one. The Gulf was one. The tide data, which he checked each evening with a ritual attention she had initially found endearing and had gradually come to understand was not endearing but necessary, in the way that medication was necessary: not a pleasure but a requirement. The folder in the second drawer of the desk, which she had seen once and filed away.

These subjects were not forbidden. Frank had never made them forbidden, had never responded to her questions with deflection or hostility or the emotional weather of a man guarding a secret. He had responded with accuracy. The accuracy was the problem; she had come to understand that accuracy was the instrument, that a man could be entirely accurate and entirely incomplete, and that she had been receiving accurate information about the house for twelve years without receiving the information the accuracy was designed to route around.

She had known this was happening.

Not known in the sense of having the facts; she had not had the facts. Known in the sense of having read the shape of the space where the facts were not, the way you read the shape of a room in the dark by the quality of the air and the resistance of the floor. She had been moving through this room in the dark for twelve years and she had learned its dimensions without ever turning on the light.

This had been, she understood, a choice.

She was less clear about why she had made it.

* * *

There had been one evening, in the spring of 2026, when she had come very close.

They had been sitting on the deck after dinner, which was something they did when the weather permitted: the Gulf in the early evening, the quality of the light in March, which was the best month. Frank had his phone, which he sometimes checked in the evenings, the tide data, and she had her book, which she had not been reading. She had been watching him read his phone with the attention she brought to things she was trying to understand.

He had a way of receiving bad news from data. She had observed it across thirty years: a very slight stilling, not distress but the adjustment of a person recalibrating an internal estimate. He had made this adjustment that evening, reading his phone. It had lasted perhaps two seconds and he had put the phone down and looked at the Gulf with the expression she associated with the territory she had been navigating around.

She had lowered her book.

She had said his name.

He had turned to look at her with the attentiveness he always brought to his name in her voice; forty years of a particular quality of attention, the way he oriented toward her when she spoke to him, which was one of the things she had loved earliest and most consistently about him.

She had looked at his face.

The question was there, on the threshold of available. It was a simple question. It had been forming for three years at that point, in various iterations, and in this version it was something like: what are you not telling me about this house. She could feel the shape of it, the way you felt a word on the tip of your tongue: present, precise, almost there.

She had looked at his face and had felt, with the clarity of a woman who had been reading rooms for thirty years, that the question was available to be asked and that asking it would be the right thing to do and that she was not going to ask it.

She was not going to ask it because the answer, whatever it was, would come with a reckoning that she was not certain the evening could absorb. Not because the evening was fragile; their evenings were not fragile. Because the answer would require her to do something with it, and she did not yet know what she would do, and she had learned, across thirty years of institutional life, that questions whose answers required immediate action were questions you did not ask until you were ready to act.

She said instead: "The water's beautiful tonight."

He said it was.

She picked up her book.

She read, or performed reading, for the remainder of the evening, and felt, in the way he was still beside her, that he had understood what she had not asked, and that his stillness was not relief but something more complicated: the stillness of a man who had been prepared to answer and had not been required to, and who was now sitting with the weight of that preparation having been unnecessary.

She had not thought about this for a long time.

She thought about it now.

* * *

The kitchen on the Tuesday he came back from Washington.

She had been cutting an apple. She had finished the cut before she turned. She had read him in the moment of turning and had understood, before he spoke, that something had changed in the register of what he was carrying. She had offered him an easier sentence.

She had understood, at the time, that she was offering an easier sentence; she had not been unaware of this. What she had not understood, until now, sitting in the week after the third flood with the accumulated weight of twelve years of not-asking rearranging itself into a pattern she had not previously assembled, was what the easier sentence had made possible.

It had not only protected him.

She had been protecting herself. She had been deciding, in the kitchen that Tuesday evening and on the deck in March 2026 and in all the other moments where the question had been available and she had chosen the lateral sentence or the adjacent topic or the turn away that kept the thing unasked, what she was willing to receive. She had been managing not only the weather of the house but the weather of her own knowledge. She had been deciding, each time, that tonight was not the night she was ready to know what there was to know.

She had been right that she was not ready.

She was less certain she had been right to keep not being ready for twelve years.

This was not a comfortable thought. She did not have the sentence for it that would make it comfortable; she was a woman who had always been able to find the sentence, the formulation, the way of naming a thing that held it at the right distance for examination, and this thought did not have that sentence. It was simply present, in the way certain thoughts were present: unmanageable, precise, requiring something she had not yet determined.

* * *

She stood at the kitchen window on the Sunday evening after Deja and Marcus had left.

The Gulf was doing what the Gulf did in the evening: accepting the light, distributing it, doing the thing with the color that she had never found the right word for and had stopped trying to name. She had been looking at this water for twenty-three years. She had learned to love it without reservation.

She thought about the drainage channel. The raised threshold on the office door. The tide gauge he checked each evening. The notebook in the second drawer. The careful attention of a man managing something she had been allowing him to manage, in part, because allowing him to manage it had allowed her not to have to.

She thought about the fact that she had made these allowances.

She thought about what they had cost.

Not what they had cost Frank; that was its own accounting, and she was not ready to open it. What they had cost her. Twelve years of navigating a room in the dark, developing an expertise in its dimensions, never turning on the light. Twelve years of lateral questions and easier sentences and the discipline of looking at the space adjacent to the thing she was not looking at. Six years during which she had, with considerable intelligence and considerable care, arranged not to know something she had been capable of knowing.

She was not certain that intelligence and care had been sufficient justification.

She was not certain they had been insufficient either.

She stood at the kitchen window and looked at the water and felt the sensation of a woman whose understanding of the past twelve years was rearranging itself around a piece of information she did not yet have, in the same way a sentence rearranged itself around a word you did not know but whose shape you could read from the space it left in the surrounding language.

She did not know what the word was.

She was beginning to understand that she had been choosing not to.

The Gulf accepted the last of the light.

Gloria turned from the window and went to finish the kitchen.

CHAPTER NINE:

Coral Bay, Florida · 2031

He had been walking for forty minutes.

It was the same route he walked most mornings when he was in Coral Bay: south along the coast road to the point where the barrier island was visible on clear days, then back through the neighborhood, the houses he had watched change across twenty-three years, the ones that had been sold and the ones that had adapted and the ones that stood unchanged in ways that were either brave or uninformed. He had been reading the neighborhood.

He had been walking it differently this week.

Since Deja had found the folder, he had been walking with the attention of a man waiting for the next thing to happen. Not dread, exactly; something more neutral. The attentiveness of a person who understands that an event has been set in motion and is waiting, with professional patience, to learn its shape.

He came around the last corner and saw both cars in the driveway.

He slowed.

Deja's car was not supposed to be there. She had left on Sunday. He had watched her go, and she had not looked back, and it was now Tuesday morning, and her car was in his driveway.

He stood on the pavement for a moment.

Then he went inside.

* * *

The house was very quiet.

Not the quiet of an empty house; a different quality, the quiet of a house in which people were present and not speaking. He stood in the hallway and listened and heard nothing and understood from the nothing that whatever was happening was happening in the kitchen.

He had been a FDRA Regional Director for eleven years. He had managed disasters. He knew the difference between the quiet before something and the quiet after it, and he knew which one this was.

He walked to the kitchen doorway.

They were at the table.

Gloria on the near side, facing him, her hands around a cup she was not drinking from. Deja on the far side, not facing him, looking at the table. Between them, in the center of the table, a folder he recognized.

He had kept that folder in the second drawer of his desk for twelve years.

He stood in the doorway.

Gloria looked at him.

She did not say anything. She was doing what she always did when she was reading a situation: receiving, without giving anything back yet. He had watched her do this across forty years in rooms where things were being decided, and he had always admired it, and he admired it now in the particular terrible way you admired something being used against you.

Deja did not look up.

He came into the kitchen.

* * *

He sat.

Not in his usual chair; there was no usual chair in this configuration, the folder on the table rearranging the room's geometry the way a significant object rearranged a room. He sat in the chair that was available, which was at the end of the table, equidistant from both of them.

The folder was between them.

He had a very precise understanding of what the folder contained, which was two hundred and twelve pages of data and methodology and projection ranges and policy recommendations and his name on the cover page in the institutional format that federal documents used, and which also contained, though this was not in any formal sense part of its contents, twelve years of a marriage conducted in the presence of information he had not shared.

He looked at Gloria.

She was looking back at him with the quality of attention she had brought to him for forty years: direct, measuring, not hostile, waiting to understand what she was looking at. He had been the subject of this attention for four decades and he had never found it comfortable, and he had never wanted her to stop.

"Deja came this morning," Gloria said.

He nodded.

"She brought this."

Gloria put her hand on the folder. Not to open it; she had clearly already been through it, or through enough of it to understand what it was. Just to indicate it. To place it formally in the conversation.

He nodded again.

"I see," he said. Which was all he had.

* * *

They sat for a moment.

The kitchen clock. The sound of the Gulf through the window, which was present every morning and which Frank had been listening to for twenty-three years and which today had a quality he could not account for, as if the same sound were arriving from a different distance.

Deja had not moved. She was looking at the table with the focused stillness of someone who had completed a task and was now waiting for the task to produce its consequences. She had brought the folder. She had placed it on the table. She had been here when Gloria looked through it. She had done what she had decided to do and she was now, in her own way, refusing to manage what came next.

He understood this. He had given her this.

Gloria was still looking at him.

He met her eyes and held them. He had a great deal of practice holding Gloria's gaze; forty years of mornings and evenings and the sustained attention of a long marriage, the looking that was different from looking at things, that was a form of communication he had never fully translated into words because the words were never quite adequate to it.

She said his name.

Not as a question. As a designation: the name she used when she was addressing him directly, when the lateral sentences had been set aside and she was speaking to the person and not the situation.

He waited.

* * *

"Who were you protecting?"

The question arrived in the kitchen the way certain things arrived in rooms: without announcement, filling the available space before anyone had registered it was coming.

Frank looked at her.

She had not asked: why didn't you tell me. She had not asked: how long have you known. She had not asked: what were you thinking. She had read the folder, or enough of it, and she was a woman of forty years of professional intelligence and she had arrived at the question that was underneath all those other questions, the one that required an answer before any of the others could be answered.

Who were you protecting.

It contained everything: the house, the twelve years, the drainage channel, the notebook in the second drawer, the easier sentences across a thousand evenings. The question asked him to account for the architecture of what he had done; not the facts of it, which were in the folder, but the logic of it, the reason he had constructed a version of their life together that he alone could see clearly.

He opened his mouth.

He had no answer.

Not because he lacked one; he had been carrying an answer for twelve years, in various forms, as the justification for every choice the folder represented. He had been protecting the house. He had been protecting the life they had built. He had been protecting the warmth of a lit kitchen at the end of a day and Gloria's shelf above the window and Deja handing him bolts on a Saturday in April 1999 and the proof of a life assembled with care. He had been protecting the thing that leaving would have required him to admit was not protectable.

All of this was true. He could say all of it.

He could not say it to Gloria, in this kitchen, with the folder on the table between them, because saying it to her now would require him to also say: and I decided that my need to protect those things was more important than your right to know what was happening to them. He could not assemble that sentence. He had never been able to assemble that sentence. It was the sentence that had been waiting behind every easier sentence for twelve years, and it was no more available now than it had ever been.

He looked at his hands.

They were steady. That was still the problem.

"Gloria," he said.

She waited.

He had nothing after her name.

She looked at him for a long time. He did not look away. He owed her that much: to be looked at and not retreat from it.

Deja had not moved.

* * *

Then Gloria did something he had not expected.

She put her hand on the folder again: the same gesture as before, placing it in the conversation. But this time she picked it up.

She stood.

She carried it to the counter and set it down, face down, so the cover page was no longer visible.

She came back to the table.

She sat.

She picked up her cup and drank from it and set it down.

"I'm going to stay," she said. "This season. I'm not deciding about after."

Frank looked at her.

"Not because of the house," she said. She said it carefully, the way she said things she had been formulating for a while. "Because I need to understand what happened. Who you've been, while I was standing next to you."

He received this.

It was not forgiveness. He understood this; he was not a man who confused things for what they were not, and this was not forgiveness. It was something different and, in some ways, harder: the decision of a woman who was choosing to stay in proximity to a man she no longer fully recognized, in order to understand who he was.

Her staying was no longer loyalty to the place.

It was something closer to an investigation.

"All right," he said.

She nodded.

Deja looked up. She looked at her mother and then at her father and then at the folder on the counter and then at the table. Her face had the expression of a structural engineer who has assessed a load-bearing thing and understands what it will and will not hold.

She said nothing.

After a while she stood and rinsed her cup at the sink and said she needed to get back. She kissed her mother on the cheek. She put her hand briefly on Frank's shoulder, on the way past, without stopping.

He felt the weight of her hand.

It was not a reassurance. It was an acknowledgement: of the thing he had given her to carry, and of the fact that she was carrying it, and of the fact that they were both, now, carrying it together, and that neither of them had chosen this arrangement.

The door.

Her car in the driveway.

Gone.

* * *

Gloria did not move for a while.

Frank sat at the table and watched her not move and understood that she was doing what she always did when she had received something she needed to process: holding still, letting it settle, not rushing the understanding.

He had always loved this about her. He was aware of this even now.

He thought about saying something. He had things he could say; inadequate things, incomplete things, the closest available approximations of what he actually wanted to say, which was something he had never found the language for and which he was beginning to understand he might never find, because the language would have required him to be a different version of himself than the one he had been for twelve years, and he did not know if that version was accessible anymore.

He did not say anything.

The Gulf was audible through the open window. The particular Tuesday morning quality of the light in the kitchen: the west windows not yet receiving the full sun, the room in its morning register, which was the register of ordinary days.

Gloria stood.

She picked up the folder from the counter.

She looked at it for a moment.

She put it on the shelf above the window, beside the ceramic bowl and the photograph of her mother and the glass bottle from their honeymoon.

Frank looked at the shelf.

He had built that shelf. It was the shelf that had been the first sign, twenty-three years ago, that Gloria was making the house her own. He had watched her put things on it across two decades; had watched it become, over time, the inventory of a woman who knew what she needed around her. He had never put anything on it. It was her shelf.

She had put his folder on her shelf.

He did not know what this meant. He had a great deal of professional experience in the interpretation of significant gestures, and he was not certain he was equipped to interpret this one. He was not certain she intended it to be interpreted. He was not certain she had known, when she did it, what she was doing.

He sat at the kitchen table and looked at the folder on the shelf, beside the ceramic bowl and the photograph of her mother and the glass bottle from their honeymoon, and he felt the quality of a room that had just changed its internal architecture in a way that would not be visible to anyone who had not been paying attention for forty years.

Gloria moved to the window.

She looked at the Gulf.

He watched her look at it.

After a while she said: "Do you want coffee?"

He looked at her.

She was still facing the window. He could not see her face.

"Yes," he said. "Thank you."

She filled the kettle.

The kitchen continued.

CHAPTER TEN:

Coral Bay, Florida · 2031

In the weeks after the kitchen table, Frank did not know what to do with his mornings.

This was a practical problem as much as an interior one. He had structured his mornings for twelve years around the rigorous discipline of a man managing something: the tide gauge before breakfast, the notebook in the second drawer, the folder in the second position from the bottom, the periodic review of the data against the projections to confirm that the projections were holding. The structure had not been onerous. It had been simply the shape of a morning: the way a man who understood that he was living in the path of something made himself useful to the fact, even in private, even when being useful to it meant only that he continued to measure it and record it.

He had checked the tide gauge on the morning of the fourth flood, which had come in October, and had found himself standing on the deck with the gauge in his hand and nothing to do with the reading.

The reading was what it was. He knew what it meant. He had known what it meant for twelve years. The difference was that the meaning was no longer a private fact. Gloria knew the gauge existed. Gloria knew why he checked it. The folder was on the shelf above the kitchen window, between the ceramic bowl and the photograph of her mother. The private accounting had become, at some point between the kitchen table and the fourth flood, something that belonged to the household rather than to him alone.

He recorded the reading in the notebook.

He put the notebook away.

He went inside and made coffee.

* * *

He had expected, he realized, to feel worse.

Not that he felt well; he was not confused about the state of things. The marriage was in the condition of a marriage that had survived something it had not been designed to survive and was in the process of determining whether survival was sufficient. Gloria moved through the house with him with the particular quality of attention she had had since the kitchen table: present, functional, occasionally warm and also engaged in something he could not fully see, a private reckoning she was conducting in parallel with their ordinary life. He could feel its presence the way he had always been able to feel the presence of things she had not yet decided to say.

He did not press her. He did not have the standing to press her. He was a man who had just had his standing in the marriage substantially revised, and he understood this with the professional clarity of someone who had spent thirty years assessing structural damage: you did not challenge the assessment, you worked with what the assessment gave you.

What it gave him was this: her continued presence, her continued willingness to be in rooms with him, her occasional hand on his arm when she passed him in the kitchen, which was a gesture so small and so familiar that he had almost missed, the first time it happened after the table, what it cost her to make it.

He had not missed it.

He had stood in the kitchen with her hand on his arm and felt something he had no precise language for, which was approximately the quality of receiving something you understood you had not earned and could not repay but which was being given anyway, for reasons that had to do with forty years of a life together and a shelf above a window and a woman who had decided, without being asked, that the person he had been was not the only version of him available.

He was not certain she was right. He was not in a position to argue.

* * *

The difficulty, which he had not anticipated, was not guilt.

Guilt would have been, in a strange way, easier; guilt had a grammar, a sequence of recognizable states, a direction of travel. What he had instead was something more like disorientation. The disorientation of a man whose interior architecture had been organized around a fixed point for twelve years, and who was now, with the fixed point gone, uncertain of his orientation.

He had known, for twelve years, exactly where the report was. He had known, at any given moment, the exact distance between his family's understanding of their situation and his own. He had known the shape of what was not being said and the precise effort required to continue not saying it. He had known, in other words, the exact dimensions of the space he was living in.

The space had changed. He could no longer read its dimensions.

This was not a complaint. He understood that the change was the correct change; that the twelve years of his orientation to the world had been purchased at a cost he had not been authorized to charge. He understood this. He simply did not yet know how to be a person who was not managing the distance between what he knew and what the people he loved knew, because he had been that person for so long that the management had become the structure of how he moved through days.

He found himself, in the first weeks, straightening things that did not need straightening.

He found himself checking the tide gauge twice.

He found himself, on a Tuesday morning in November, standing in the office with his hand on the second drawer, not opening it, because the folder was on the shelf in the kitchen now and there was nothing in the second drawer that required his attention and he had come into the office out of habit and the habit had arrived without its content.

He stood there for a moment.

Then he went to find Gloria.

* * *

Isaiah came for Thanksgiving.

He was sixteen now. He had been fifteen the morning of the third flood, moving the car to higher ground with the boredom of a teenager executing a procedure he had done before, and he was sixteen at Thanksgiving, and the difference was not dramatic but it was present: something in him had settled into a register that was no longer adolescent in the particular way of unformed things. He was still private. He was still oriented outward, in the way Frank had always read him, toward the world rather than the room. But there was a quality of decision in it now that had not been there before; the sense of a person who had chosen his orientation rather than simply having it.

Frank watched him across Thanksgiving dinner with the intent attention he had always brought to Isaiah and that he brought now with an additional quality he could not entirely name. Something close to recognition. The quality of watching a person who reminded you of yourself in a way that was not comfortable.

Isaiah was building an exit. Frank had understood this for two years, in the way he understood the things Isaiah did not say, by the shape of what he avoided: the conversations about the future of the house, the questions about staying that were always slightly too careful, the notebook he kept and did not leave lying around. He was a fifteen-year-old who was already, quietly and without announcement, arranging his departure. Frank had watched him do this and had felt, each time, the simultaneous pride and grief of watching someone you love, choose correctly.

He watched him at the table and thought - he does not know yet what he is already carrying.

Not the report; Deja had said nothing to Isaiah, and Frank did not know yet whether she would or when. Not the specifics. But the shape. The particular shape of a family that had been living inside something it had not named, and the way that living left marks on everyone in the house, including the people who had not been in the room when the thing was named.

Isaiah would find out eventually. Frank was not certain when or how. He was certain that when Isaiah found out, he would have been carrying the shape of it for years already, without knowing it had a name.

Not the report, not the twelve years, not the easier sentences and the lateral questions. The inheritance. The exact texture of knowledge he had given his family without their consent, not by telling them, but by the way the concealment had shaped every room they had all been in together.

He had given Isaiah this. Without intending to. Without being able to undo it.

Isaiah passed him the bread without being asked.

Frank took it and said thank you and they did not look at each other with any particular significance, because that was not the register Isaiah used, and Frank had been watching him long enough to know when not to look for significance.

* * *

He understood it clearly for the first time in December.

He had been out to check the gauge, which was a habit he had not abandoned and which he was no longer certain was a measurement or simply a movement; the act of going to the gauge having lost its original function and not yet acquired a new one. He stood on the deck with the reading in his hand and the Gulf in front of him and the December light doing the thing it did in December, which was to be clear and flat and specific, the light that showed you what was there without the mediation of heat or haze.

He had stood on this deck for twenty-three years.

He had stood on it the morning of the third flood, and the morning of the second, and the morning of the first, and on a summer morning in 2024 with Amara asleep on his chest, and on the Tuesday evening he came back from Washington with the reclassification already in motion, and on hundreds of other mornings across twelve years, each one carrying the same private knowledge, the same private measurement, the same awareness of what the water was doing and what it would continue to do.

He thought about the decision on the I-95, twelve years ago.

He had told himself, for twelve years, that he had not made a decision on the I-95. He had told himself that the silence was a deferral, a waiting for the right moment, a reasonable delay in the delivery of information that would eventually be delivered. He had told himself this in the way you told yourself things that were necessary to continue functioning, and he had functioned, and the silence had continued, and the right moment had never arrived.

He could see now, standing on the deck in the December light, that the silence had not been a deferral.

The silence had been a decision. It had been made not in one moment but across a sequence of small failures to act, across a thousand evenings where the information was available and he had not delivered it, across the specific gravity of a moving car and a dimming phone screen and a lit kitchen and a tired woman who had offered him an easier sentence and he had taken it.

He had taken it.

That was the decision. Not the conference room, not the I-95, not the drainage channel or the notebook in the second drawer or the folder in the second position from the bottom. Not any one of those things. All of them together, each one the decision not to make the decision, accumulated across twelve years into a structure he had mistaken for a circumstance.

He had built it. He had maintained it. He had lived inside it.

He stood on the deck and held this understanding and found that it did not produce what he had always assumed it would produce if he ever arrived at it directly: it did not produce the anguish of a man confronting a moral failure. It produced something quieter and, in some ways, harder. The quality of a man who has understood something he cannot now unknow, and who must determine what to do with the understanding now that the thing it describes is already over.

The secret was no longer his to keep. Not because he had chosen to release it. Because Deja had found the folder and brought it to the kitchen table and events had taken the choice away from him, in the way events took choices away when you had deferred them long enough.

The weight he had carried for forty years had passed to Gloria and Deja.

They would carry it differently. He did not yet know how. He understood that he would spend the remainder of his time in this house watching how they carried it, and that this watching would be its own kind of reckoning, and that he did not have the right to make it easier for them than it actually was.

He put the gauge reading in his pocket.

He stood for a moment longer.

The Gulf was what it was. The barrier islands were where they were. The water was at the level it was at, which was the level it had been moving toward for twenty-three years and which it would continue to move toward with the complete indifference of a physical process, which had no interest in what Frank Alderman had or had not done about it.

He did not know what the water was going to do next.

This was new. For twelve years he had known, with a precision that was both his professional achievement and his private burden, exactly what the water was going to do. He had known the projections, the timelines, the confidence intervals, the median and the seventy-fifth percentile and the appendix he had told the room in Washington contained the worst-case scenarios. He had known all of it. The knowing had been the architecture of everything.

He did not know anymore. Not because the data had changed; the data was what it was. But the data was no longer only his. It was on the shelf in the kitchen, between Gloria's bowl and her mother's photograph. It was in

Deja's possession, in whatever form she had decided to hold it. It was in the household now, distributed across the people who had been living inside its consequences without his permission, and his individual knowledge of it was no longer the structure that was holding anything up.

He was standing in the present tense for the first time in twelve years.

He did not know what to do with the present tense.

He stood on the deck and looked at the water and waited to find out.

* * *

That evening Gloria made the grouper.

He had not asked for it; she had simply made it, the particular grouper with the rice and the garden salad that she had made on the Tuesday he came back from Washington twelve years ago, that she had made periodically across the intervening years as a thing she made because she knew he liked it, without particular ceremony.

He ate it at the kitchen table and watched her across the table and understood that he was watching something he had watched a thousand times across forty years and that he was watching it differently now; not more clearly, exactly, but from a different position, the position of a man who had lost the elevated vantage of private knowledge and was now, finally, simply present in the room.

She talked about Deja's project. About Isaiah's school. About whether they should replace the deck boards in the spring or wait another season.

He said what he thought. He said the deck boards could wait.

She disagreed. She said the third flood had taken more out of them than the second and she would rather do it in the spring.

He said all right.

She smiled briefly at her plate.

They washed up after. He washed; she dried. The arrangement of twenty-three years in this kitchen. The particular domestic choreography of two people who knew which way each other moved.

She put the last thing away and folded the towel and hung it on the rail and said she was going to read for a while.

"All right," he said.

She touched his arm on the way past. The small gesture, the one that cost her something. He stayed very still while she did it and did not say anything because there was nothing he could say that was adequate to it - and he had learned, across ten chapters of Frank Alderman's education in what he had done to the people who loved him, that the adequate thing was sometimes simply to receive.

He heard her go upstairs.

He stood in the kitchen for a while.

He looked at the shelf above the window: the ceramic bowl, the photograph of her mother, the glass bottle from their honeymoon, and the folder between them, face out now, its title visible in the kitchen light.

COASTAL RESIDENTIAL OBSOLESCENCE: A 30-YEAR PROJECTION.

His name below it, in the institutional format of federal documents.

He looked at his name.

He had spent twelve years protecting the document from view. It had been in a drawer. It had been a private fact. It was now on a shelf in his kitchen, visible to anyone who came through the door, available to the household in the way that Gloria's bowl and her mother's photograph were available: as a thing that belonged here, that had been placed here by someone who had decided it belonged here, that was part of the inventory of this room.

He did not know if he would ever fully understand what she had meant by putting it there.

He turned off the kitchen light.

He went upstairs.

He was, for the first time in twelve years, a man without a secret.

He did not yet know what kind of man that was.

He went to find out.

PART TWO ISAIAH

CHAPTER ELEVEN:

Coral Bay, Florida · 2045

The water was warmer than he expected.

Not warm exactly; ankle-deep in November, the Gulf did what it did in November, which was to be several degrees cooler than the air. But warmer than it should have been for this time of year, and he noticed this the way he noticed temperatures, automatically, as data that updated his working model of a system he had been tracking for seven years.

He was standing where the front porch had been.

He was fairly certain of this. He had cross-referenced the property survey from the county records against the current bathymetric data before driving down, and he had walked the line of the seawall remnant, which was still visible as a low concrete edge running along what had been the eastern property boundary, and he had paced the distance from there. The porch had been here, or close enough to here that the difference didn't matter for what he had come to do.

He wasn't certain what he had come to do.

He had driven four hours. He had told his colleague Priya he was doing a site visit in the corridor, which was true enough; Coral Bay was in the corridor, the data for this stretch of coast was in his dataset, he had professional reasons to be standing in a shallow inlet on a Tuesday in November. He had not told Priya that this inlet had a street grid under it, or that one of the addresses in the grid was the one he had grown up visiting at Christmas and Easter and the occasional summer week when his mother needed coverage and his grandparents had said of course, bring him.

He looked at the water.

It was clear enough to see the bottom: the pale sand, the occasional piece of concrete, the ghost of a curb line running east to west about ten feet in front of him. The neighborhood was still readable if you knew how to read it. He knew how to read it; this was, in a precise sense, his job.

* * *

He took his phone out.

The photograph was where he had put it, in the camera roll, dated summer 2024. He had been two years old in the summer of 2024 and he had no memory of the photograph being taken, but his mother had sent it to him three years ago when he started working on Gulf Coast displacement data, because she thought he should have it. He had looked at it when it arrived and filed it without examining it - and then he had come across it again six months later when he was looking for something else - and had looked at it for longer.

The house. The deck. His grandfather on the deck with something in a carrier on his chest, which he knew from other photographs had been him.

He raised the phone.

He tried to frame the photograph against what was actually here - the inlet, the pale sand, the ghost of the curb, the open sky where the house had been. The gesture of a person trying to overlay two images that no longer shared a coordinate system.

They didn't align.

He had known they wouldn't. He lowered the phone. He looked at the photograph for a moment longer - the house, perfect and still in the summer light, the blue-green water behind it, his grandfather's hand resting on the back of the small sleeping weight on his chest.

He put the phone in his pocket.

* * *

He had been to forty-three sites in the past three years.

Not all of them were like this; most of the sites in his dataset were properties that had been sold, or condemned, or relocated, where the structures still stood in various states of managed decline. The inundated sites were a subset. Of those, the ones where the inundation was complete and the original footprint was fully submerged were rarer. He had been to eleven of those, including this one.

The other ten he had moved through with the professional attention he brought to field work: reading the bathymetric data against the survey records, noting the rate and pattern of inundation, recording observations in his notebook. He was good at this. He had been doing it long enough that the data and the landscape had become a single language; he no longer had to translate between them.

This site he was reading differently.

Not incorrectly, he was still reading it. He could see the drainage pattern from the remnant curbing, could estimate the timeline of inundation from the sediment distribution, could note the temperature of the water as data in his working model. He was doing all of this. He was also doing something else, a second reading running parallel to the professional one, using a different instrument.

He did not have a precise name for the instrument.

It was something like a place that had been inhabited and loved, readable as a residue even after the inhabitation was over. He had felt it at some of the other sites too, the ones where the inundation was recent enough that the neighborhood had not yet fully resolved into geography. A feeling adjacent to presence. The after of a place that had been a somewhere.

This site had it more than the others.

He stood in the water and let that register without examining why.

* * *

He was standing the way his grandfather stood at water.

He noticed this without intending to; weight forward, arms loose at his sides, eyes tracking the surface. He had photographs of his grandfather in this posture, on the deck of this house, across multiple years; he had grown up seeing the posture and had apparently absorbed it without noticing, the way you absorbed the grammar of a household before you had words for grammar.

His grandfather had died four years ago. Seventy-five, the end of a long decline that had been, as his mother described it, peaceful in the way of things that had been prepared for over a long time. Isaiah had been in the field in Louisiana when it happened and had driven back and arrived at the house that was no longer the Coral Bay house, the smaller house his grandparents had moved to after the fourth flood, and had sat in the living room with his mother and grandmother and said the things that were available to be said.

He had not known his grandfather well, exactly. He had known him across visits and holidays and the occasional longer stretch, and he had been aware, from an early age, of the quality of his grandfather's attention: precise, professional, slightly in excess of what the situation seemed to require. His grandfather watched things the way Isaiah watched things. He had assumed this was coincidence, the way certain gestures moved through families without anyone choosing to pass them on.

He was less certain of this now, standing in the water of what had been his grandfather's street.

He had been less certain of a number of things since he started working in this corridor.

* * *

There was something his family did not discuss.

He had known this since childhood, not as a fact but as a texture: the unique feel of certain conversations that ended at a set point, certain rooms that changed register when certain subjects approached, certain questions his mother had deflected with the efficiency of a structural engineer redirecting load. He had grown up inside this texture the way you grew up inside weather: without choosing it, without naming it, with only the accumulated knowledge of how to move through it.

He did not know what it was.

He had theories. Not formal theories; more like the preliminary observation stage before a hypothesis, the noticing that something was present before determining what it was. There had been a period, when he was fifteen or sixteen, when he had thought it was simply the house: the tension of a family that disagreed about whether to stay in a place that was becoming untenable. His mother had clearly thought they should leave. His grandmother had wanted to stay. His grandfather had been harder to read.

He had moved on from that theory.

The tension had not resolved when they left the Coral Bay house. It had simply changed shape. His mother had carried something after the third flood that she had not carried before; he had not known what it was and had not asked, because he had learned, inside the grammar of this household, that asking directly about the thing that was present was not the way the household worked. You approached laterally. You waited. You let things arrive in their own form.

Things had not yet arrived in their form.

He was twenty-nine. He was standing in the inlet that had been his grandparents' street, reading a professional dataset that included this address among forty-three others, and whatever his household had been organized around for the first eighteen years of his life was still somewhere in the background of his understanding, present and unnamed.

He was, he thought, in the preliminary observation stage.

* * *

He stayed for a while.

There was no correct amount of time. He knew this. He was a researcher and he understood that the impulse to stay at a site for a right amount of time was an impulse without a rational basis; the data did not care how long he stood in it, the bathymetry was not improved by his presence, the sediment distribution was not altered by the quality of his attention. He stayed anyway.

The light was doing the December thing on the Gulf: flat, clear, specific, showing you what was there.

He thought about his grandfather on the deck of this house, in this light, checking the tide gauge each evening before bed. His mother had mentioned this once, offhandedly, in the way she mentioned things she had not decided how to classify. He had filed it. He filed most things. He had been filing things about this family for twenty-nine years and had not yet determined the complete shape of what he was filing them toward.

He turned.

He walked back through the water toward the seawall remnant, unhurried, careful on the uneven sand. He reached the concrete edge and sat and put his shoes back on: both shoes, both knots, the deliberate, unhurried attention of a person who did not need to be anywhere in the next few minutes

He stood.

He had his notebook in his jacket pocket. A researcher's notebook, well-used, the spine slightly cracked from being opened flat. He did not take it out.

Whatever he had come here to understand, he had not finished understanding it. Writing it down before it was finished would close it too early. He had learned this; it was one of the few things about his work he considered a genuine methodological principle rather than a preference.

You recorded when you knew what you were recording.

He did not yet know.

He walked toward the road.

He did not look back.

* * *

He sat in the car for a few minutes before starting it.

The dataset was open on his laptop on the passenger seat, the Gulf Coast corridor, forty-three addresses in various states of inundation or managed decline. He looked at the address for this property: 114 Halcyon Drive, Coral Bay, FL. Inundation complete, 2039. Prior ownership: F. and G. Alderman, 1998-2036. Current status: submerged, no structures remaining.

He had looked at this entry before. Many times; it was in his dataset and he worked with his dataset daily and the entry was simply an entry, a row in a table, one of forty-three. He had not flagged it, had not noted the prior ownership in any of his working documents, had not done anything that distinguished it from the other forty-two.

He looked at it now.

F. and G. Alderman.

His grandfather's name, in his professional dataset, abbreviated to an initial and a surname in the way that property records abbreviated names, making them legible as administrative facts rather than as people.

He had known the address was in the dataset. He had put it there himself, when he built the corridor inventory, because it was in the corridor and it met the criteria and his work did not make exceptions for personal connection. He was methodologically committed to this. The data was the data.

He had not, until today, stood in it.

He closed the laptop.

He started the car.

He pulled out of what had been the car park at the end of what had been the street and drove north, back toward the city, back toward his apartment and his work and the corridor dataset with forty-three entries, one of which had a name in it that he had been passing over for three years without fully stopping.

He did not know yet what stopping would mean.

He drove north.

The Gulf moved alongside him for a while, visible between the buildings and the trees, doing what it always did, which was to be present and indifferent and entirely without interest in what Isaiah Alderman-Cross had understood or not understood on a Tuesday in November while standing in water that had been, before it was water, a street, and before it was a street, a place where someone he loved had stood in the same posture, watching.

CHAPTER TWELVE:

Tampa, Florida · 2045

The dataset had 847 entries.

He had built it over three years, pulling from county property records, FDRA flood maps, insurance filings, the longitudinal displacement surveys his organization ran out of the University of South Florida, and the bathymetric data that the NOAA maintained for the Gulf Coast corridor. Each entry was an address: a property that had been inundated, condemned, relocated, or abandoned in the period between 2025 and 2044. Each entry had a status code, a timeline, a prior ownership record, and a set of fields he had added himself because the standard survey instruments did not capture what he wanted to know, which was not only whether people had left but how they had left: what the decision had looked like, what had accelerated it, what had delayed it.

He was interested in the delay.

Most of the research in this space focused on the decision to leave as an outcome: you modelled the factors that predicted departure, you ran the regressions, you produced the coefficient table. He had done this work and found it incomplete in a way he had spent two years trying to specify. The factors predicted departure in aggregate. They did not explain the texture of why particular households delayed for years past the rational threshold, past the point where the calculus of staying was obviously negative, sometimes past the point of safe exit.

He had a hypothesis about this. He was still building the evidence.

* * *

His office was a shared space on the fourth floor of the Institute building.

He had a desk by the window, which looked out over the bay rather than the street, which he had specifically requested and which his supervisor Priya had arranged without comment, understanding, as she understood most things, what he was actually asking for. The bay was not the Gulf; it was enclosed, managed, monitored by the port authority's sensor network. But it was water with a horizon, and he worked better with a horizon in his peripheral vision. This was not something he had articulated to Priya; it was something she had read from the way he oriented himself in rooms.

Priya Chen was forty-four, a geographer by training who had spent fifteen years in displacement research across four countries before joining the Institute. She was the most methodologically rigorous person Isaiah had worked with, which was not the same as the most imaginative, though she was also that. She had a specific way of reading his draft reports: she would print them out, sit at her own desk, and read without a pen. Then she would come to his desk with a single question. The question was never about the findings. It was always about the architecture - about the category he had assumed rather than tested, the variable he had controlled for in a way that closed off the thing he was actually interested in.

He had learned more from Priya's single questions than from most other professional experiences combined.

He was not thinking about Priya. He was looking at the delay data.

* * *

The delay data was the part of the dataset that most people were not looking at.

The standard framing of climate displacement treated delay as a measurement problem: if you had better data, better outreach, better early warning systems, you could reduce the delay between rational departure threshold and actual departure, and fewer people would be caught by the event they had stayed too long for. This framing was not wrong. It was also, Isaiah had come to believe, not quite right.

What the delay data showed, when you looked at it longitudinally and with the granularity of property-level records rather than aggregate survey responses, was this: delay was not randomly distributed across the population of households that had crossed the rational threshold. It was concentrated in certain household types, and the types it was most concentrated in were not the ones the literature predicted.

The literature predicted delay in low-income households facing resource constraints. Financial barriers to relocation, lack of information, limited social networks in receiving communities. All real, all documented, all well-theorized.

The delay he kept finding was in a different population: mid-to-high income households, often with professional members who had direct access to the relevant data, in properties with long tenure, with strong social ties to the place, and with a family structure that included at least one older member who had either built the property or arrived in it in their thirties or earlier.

This was the part of his hypothesis he had not yet written down in a form he was willing to share.

Households, in other words, where someone knew.

* * *

He worked with the property records the way he worked with field sites: by reading them until they stopped being records and became places.

This was not a standard methodological position. The standard position was the opposite: you worked with the records until the places stopped being places and became data, legible, comparable, amenable to the operations that produced findings. He did both. He had learned to do both because neither alone was sufficient for what he was trying to understand.

The records gave him the facts: tenure, ownership, sale date, insurance status, flood event timeline. The facts were the skeleton. What he was interested in was the flesh: the texture of how a household had occupied a property across time, which was not in the records but was sometimes readable between them, in the gaps between sale dates and flood events, in the sequence of insurance claims, in the pattern of improvements and repairs that showed you, if you knew how to read it, whether a household was investing in permanence or managing decline.

Most households, by the time they left, had been managing decline for years.

The managing was what interested him. Not the departure.

* * *

He had been working, for the past three weeks, on a cluster of entries in the mid-coastal corridor.

Fourteen properties, all within a half-mile radius, all showing similar delay patterns: rational threshold crossed somewhere between 2026 and 2029, actual departure between 2033 and 2038. An average delay of six years. At the high end, one household had delayed eleven years past the point where the insurance had lapsed and the flood events were annual.

He was looking at this household now.

The property record showed a single owner across thirty-one years of tenure, which was unusual in the current dataset; most long-tenure properties had transferred at least once through death or sale. This one had not. The owner had acquired the property in 1997 and had remained in the record as owner-occupant through the final flood event in 2036, at which point the property had been sold to a land trust for below-market value and the owner had relocated inland.

The insurance record showed something he had seen before but not yet theorized: a pattern of self-insurance that began around 2020, four years before the first major flood event, which was earlier than most households in the dataset. Most households moved to self-insurance reactively, after the first denial or the first prohibitive premium. This one had moved proactively.

He noted this.

He did not yet know what to do with it. That was fine; he had learned, across three years of building this dataset, that the entries that resisted immediate classification were usually the ones that eventually clarified something he had been circling without landing on. He filed the observation in his notebook and moved on.

He had forty-seven more entries to review before the end of the month.

* * *

Priya came to his desk at three-thirty.

She had printed something; she had a page in her hand, which meant it was a draft of something he had written rather than something she was giving him. She stood at the side of his desk rather than pulling up a chair, which was her signal that the question would be brief.

"The delay paper," she said. "The household-type distribution."

"Yes."

"Your mid-to-high income cluster with long-tenure and professional data access." She looked at the page. "You're calling this 'informed delay.'"

"Working term," he said.

"It's good." She put the page on the desk. "But the mechanism is underspecified. You're describing who delays. You're not yet explaining why someone who has access to the data and understands what it means would delay departure beyond the rational threshold."

He looked at the page.

"You have a hypothesis about the why," she said. It was not a question.

"I have an observation," he said.

"What's the observation?"

He was quiet for a moment. The bay was doing what it did at three-thirty: the light changing in the specific way of late afternoon over water, the surface shifting from the flat gray of midday toward the beginning of the gold that would develop over the next hour.

"The properties with the longest delay," he said. "In almost every case, there's a point, somewhere in the record, where someone in the household had professional-level access to the relevant data. Not general awareness. Quantified knowledge of the timeline."

Priya waited.

"And then they stayed anyway," he said. "For years. Sometimes decades."

"And your hypothesis about why."

He looked at the bay.

"I think the knowledge changed something about what leaving meant," he said. "Not the rational calculus. Something else. Something about what it would cost to be the person who left."

Priya looked at him for a moment.

"Write that down," she said.

She took the page and went back to her desk.

He wrote it down.

* * *

He stayed late.

This was not unusual; he often stayed past six when he was inside a problem that had not resolved. The building thinned out around him, the quieting of an office floor when the day-workers left and the people who were inside something remained. He liked this hour. The dataset was more legible in it, or he was more legible to himself in it; he was not sure which.

He went back through the mid-coastal cluster.

He was looking at the proactive self-insurance entry, the one that had moved to self-insurance in 2020, four years early. He had an additional field in his dataset that he had added eighteen months ago when he realized the standard records did not capture it: a field for what he called prior knowledge indicators, which was a composite variable built from insurance adjustment timing, property improvement patterns, and any public record evidence of professional involvement in climate or flood risk work by members of the household.

He had not filled in this field for all forty-seven entries in the cluster. He had been working through them systematically.

He opened the entry.

He filled in the fields he could fill from the record: insurance adjustment, 2020, proactive, four years pre-event. Property improvements: drainage work, 2019, garage. Elevation threshold modification, 2018, office door. The pattern of improvements of a household that was preparing rather than reacting.

For the prior knowledge indicator, he needed to check the professional history of the household members.

He had the owner's name from the property record.

He opened the professional registry search.

He typed the name.

He looked at the result for a moment.

Then he closed the laptop.

He sat at his desk with the closed laptop in front of him and the bay outside the window doing the evening thing, the gold fully developed now, the surface of the water catching it in the way that surfaces caught evening light when the angle was right.

He had filled in a lot of fields in this dataset.

He had not expected this one.

He sat for a while.

Then he opened the laptop again.

He left the field blank.

He closed the dataset.

He went home.

CHAPTER THIRTEEN:

Tampa, Florida · 2045

He had been building the prior knowledge indicator for six weeks.

It was the most granular part of the dataset and the most time-consuming, because the standard records did not capture it directly. You had to reconstruct it from adjacent evidence: the timing of insurance decisions, the sequence of property improvements, and whatever professional history of the household members was accessible through public registries and published research. For most entries this took twenty minutes. For entries with long tenure and professional household members in relevant fields, it took longer.

He had worked through forty-one of the forty-seven entries in the mid-coastal cluster. Six remained.

He opened the next entry.

* * *

The entry was unremarkable at first pass.

Single owner, long tenure, a property in the northern section of the corridor that had flooded three times before the household departed in 2037. The insurance record showed the standard pattern for the cluster: coverage lapses, self-insurance, the specific sequence he had come to recognize as a household managing rather than reacting. Nothing in the record that distinguished it from the others.

He moved to the prior knowledge indicator.

For the professional history field, he ran the owner's name through the standard registry. No relevant professional credentials. He ran the spouse's name. A retired educator. He noted this and moved to the next field, which was his custom field for source documentation: any published or institutional material in which the property's address or immediate corridor appeared in a predictive rather than retrospective context. Studies, reports, models, anything that would indicate that someone, somewhere, had assessed this specific area before the flood events rather than after.

He ran the corridor search.

Three results. Two were retrospective analyzes, published after the first major flood event in 2028. The third was different.

He opened it.

* * *

It was a citation in an insurance industry working paper from 2023.

The working paper was a reassessment of coastal residential risk models, produced by an actuarial team at a major insurer as part of their internal policy review. He had seen papers like this before; the insurance industry had been revisiting its Gulf Coast exposure models throughout the 2020s, and many of them cited the same small set of foundational studies. He read the citation.

It referenced an internal FDRA study from 2019. "Coastal Residential Obsolescence: A 30-Year Projection." The actuarial paper cited it for its median inundation timeline projections for the mid-coastal corridor, noting that the projections had proven, in retrospect, to be among the most accurate early assessments of the area. The citation included a brief description of the study's methodology: property-level analysis, high-confidence interval, median and seventy-fifth percentile projections for chronic inundation onset.

He noted that the study had been reclassified. The actuarial paper mentioned this in passing, as a methodological caveat: the original FDRA study was not publicly available, but its projections had circulated through institutional channels and had been cited in subsequent work. The actuarial team had accessed a copy through a congressional subcommittee disclosure process in 2024.

He had not encountered this study before.

He went to find it.

* * *

It took him forty minutes.

The congressional subcommittee disclosure was part of the public record, indexed in a federal archive he had access to through the Institute's research library subscription. The study itself had been included as an exhibit in a 2024 hearing on federal flood risk disclosure policy. He found the exhibit number. He pulled the file.

It was two hundred and twelve pages.

He read the executive summary.

The methodology was forensic. That was the word that came to him, reading it: not rigorous, which was the standard term, but forensic, in the sense of a precision applied to a material with the deliberate intention of producing something that could not be reasonably disputed. The confidence intervals were not hedged. The projections were stated as median outcomes, with the worst-case scenarios noted as available in the appendix. The language of the executive summary was plain without being imprecise: it said what it meant, it cited its basis, it did not reach beyond the data.

He had read a great deal of flood risk literature across seven years of research. This was among the best he had encountered. He noted this as he read it, the way he noted all such assessments: factually, without elaboration.

He reached the author field.

* * *

He looked at it.

One breath.

He looked at it for one breath and then he looked at the bay.

The bay was doing what it did at eleven in the morning: the light flat and working, the surface unremarkable. A container ship was moving across the middle distance, slow and enormous, doing the thing container ships did, which was to be present without requiring anything.

He looked back at the screen.

The name was still there.

F. Alderman. FDRA Regional Director. Washington D.C., 2019.

He closed the file.

* * *

He had three other entries to work through before lunch.

He opened the next one.

It was a straightforward case: a retired couple, no professional background in relevant fields, standard reactive insurance pattern, departed 2034. He filled in the fields efficiently and moved to the one after that.

He worked for forty minutes. He filled in eight fields across two entries. He noted a pattern in the drainage modification timing that he had not previously observed in this cluster and added a flag for follow-up. He was thorough. He was present in the work.

He did not go back to the file he had closed.

* * *

He ate at his desk.

Priya came by at twelve-thirty to ask whether he was going to the department seminar that afternoon. He said he had planned to. She said good, because the presenter was doing something methodologically interesting with longitudinal displacement data from the Netherlands, and she thought he should hear it.

He said he would be there.

She went back to her desk.

He looked at his lunch.

He thought about the seminar. The Netherlands data. He had been meaning to look more carefully at the Dutch corridor studies; there was a Deltares research team whose modeling he had been meaning to read for a year, and the seminar might give him an entry point. He added this to his task list.

He did not add anything about the file he had closed.

He ate his lunch.

* * *

After the seminar he went back to his desk and opened a new document.

He had been planning to write up the delay mechanism section of his paper for the past two weeks. He had the observations. He had the supporting data. He had the conversation with Priya in which he had articulated the hypothesis in its clearest form so far. He had been putting the writing off without examining why.

He started writing.

He wrote for two hours. The section came with less difficulty than he had expected; the ideas were more organized than he had realized, and the writing produced the clarifying effect that writing sometimes produced, where the act of putting things in sequence revealed the sequence's logic in a way that thinking about them had not. He wrote five pages. He felt, at the end of them, that the mechanism was finally in a form he could show Priya.

He saved the document.

He looked at his task list.

The flag he had added that morning: follow-up on drainage modification timing in the mid-coastal cluster.

The note about the Netherlands seminar. Several other items from the past week.

He looked at the task list for a moment.

He added one item: prior knowledge indicator, entry 42, complete.

He did not add anything further.

He closed the task list.

* * *

He left at six.

The building was quiet by then, the floor mostly empty. He packed his bag with the efficiency of a person who had been doing this long enough that the sequence of it was automatic: laptop, notebook, the charger he always forgot and had learned to check for last. He stood at his desk for a moment.

He looked at the bay. The evening light was doing what it did, the gold that developed each day at this hour, reliable, indifferent.

The file he had closed was still closed. It was still in the federal archive, indexed, available, part of the public record since 2024. It would be there tomorrow. It would be there the day after that. It had been there since 2024 and he had been working in this research space for three years and he had not encountered it until today, and having encountered it he had closed it, and it had remained closed for the rest of the working day.

This was, he noted without examining it, a choice.

He picked up his bag.

He went home.

CHAPTER FOURTEEN:

Tampa, Florida · 2045

He opened the file on a Sunday.

Not that Sunday meant anything particular in his week; he worked on Sundays with some regularity, and the choice of day was more a function of the quality of Sunday mornings in the apartment, which was quieter than weekday mornings in a way that was useful for certain kinds of work. But he was aware, opening it, that he had waited four days. He had not planned to wait four days. He had simply not opened it on Thursday, or Friday, or Saturday, and now it was Sunday and he was opening it.

He had finished the prior knowledge indicator for the remaining entries in the mid-coastal cluster. He had flagged the drainage modification pattern for follow-up. He had submitted the delay mechanism section to Priya, who had read it overnight and come back with her question, which was: what is the mechanism for the moment of decision - not the years of delay, but the event or non-event that finally moved the household? He had started working on this and found it harder than he expected, which usually meant he was closer to something than he had realized.

He opened the file.

* * *

He read it properly this time.

Not the executive summary; he had read that four days ago. He started at page one and read forward, the way he read any technical document that he needed to understand rather than simply cite: steadily, with the specific quality of attention that allowed the logic of a piece of work to accumulate rather than being sampled. He had learned this from Priya, who read everything this way, who said once that you could not understand an argument by reading its conclusions first, because the conclusions required the architecture behind them and the architecture was in the pages most people skipped.

The study was methodologically rigorous. He had noted this in passing when he read the executive summary, and reading the full document confirmed it. The baseline data was precisely sourced. The modeling assumptions were stated with a specificity that was unusual for internal government documents of this period; most internal studies of this era hedged their assumptions to provide cover for the recommendations, and this one did not hedge. The assumptions were stated as what they were: the best available estimates given the data, with confidence intervals attached.

He read the methodology section twice.

Not because it was unclear; because it was clear in a way he wanted to be certain of. The choice of confidence intervals, the specific decision to present median projections rather than best-case scenarios, the inclusion of the worst-case appendix with the note that these were not intended to be alarming but to be accurate: all of these were choices. Not unusual choices, in retrospect; they were the choices a careful researcher made. But they had the quality of choices that had been made deliberately, against some alternative that the researcher had considered and rejected.

He was reading a document that its author had intended to be believed.

* * *

He reached the property-level analysis on page forty-seven.

The study had broken the corridor into sub-zones and produced property-level projections for each sub-zone, which was the specific contribution that had made the actuarial paper cite it: the granularity of the projection was significantly higher than the publicly available flood maps of the period. Isaiah read through the sub-zones methodically, checking the methodology against what he now knew, from seven years of subsequent data, had actually happened.

The projections were accurate. Not approximately accurate; specifically accurate, in the way that a carefully constructed model was accurate when its assumptions were correct and its data was good and the person who built it had not introduced optimistic bias into the confidence intervals.

He found the sub-zone that contained Coral Bay.

He read the projection for this sub-zone: onset of chronic inundation within twelve to eighteen years under median conditions. The date range implied by that projection, from a 2019 baseline, was 2031 to 2037.

The first major flood event in Coral Bay had been in 2024.

The third flood, the one he remembered as the one where his family had moved through the house with the efficiency of people who had done it before, had been in 2031.

He sat with this for a moment.

The projection was conservative. The actual timeline had been faster. This was consistent with the broader pattern across the corridor: the median projections from this period had tended to understate the rate of inundation, because the sea level rise component of the models had been calibrated on data that predated the acceleration of the late 2020s. The study's projections were not wrong. They had been overtaken by conditions that were worse than median.

He noted this in his working document.

He continued reading.

* * *

He was on page ninety-three when he first noticed something.

He had been reading for two hours. The study was two hundred and twelve pages and he was moving through it steadily, and the reading had settled into the rhythm of sustained technical work, where the material became more legible as you went deeper into it because you were carrying more context for each subsequent section. He had been noting things in his working document as he read:

data points, methodology observations, the occasional comparison against more recent studies.

On page ninety-three there was a section on the specific household characteristics associated with delayed departure in the study's modelled scenarios. The study was primarily a property-level projection document, not a behavioral one, and this section was a relatively brief departure from the main argument; a three-page discussion of why the projection timelines might not translate directly into departure timelines, given what was known about household behavior under conditions of chronic rather than acute risk.

He read it carefully.

The section was written in the same plain and precise language as the rest of the document. But the plain and precise language, applied to the question of why households did not leave when the data indicated they should, produced something he had not expected: specificity about a type of household he recognized.

Long-tenure properties. Strong attachment to place. Households with professional members whose expertise gave them access to relevant data. The section did not make an argument about these households; it noted their presence in the delay literature and flagged them as a factor that could complicate the translation from projection to departure. But the noting was specific. It did not generalize.

Isaiah read the passage again.

He was not reading the report's argument. He was reading something underneath it: the way a particular kind of attention, applied to a particular kind of problem, left its mark in the specific choices of what to include and how to frame it. The section on household behavior was three pages in a two-hundred-and-twelve-page document. You did not write three pages on something unless you had thought about it.

He had spent seven years reading research documents. He knew the difference between a literature review conducted to be thorough and one conducted because the researcher had an interest in the material that exceeded the document's official scope.

He could not have said with certainty which this was.

He continued reading.

* * *

He went back to the executive summary.

He had read it four days ago and again when he opened the file this morning and he was reading it a third time now, looking at something specific: the choice to describe the projections as median rather than as probable or likely or expected. The word median was a technical term and its use was correct. It was also a choice with implications that a non-specialist reader would not necessarily catch.

Median meant the middle of the distribution. It meant that half the possible outcomes were worse. It meant that if you told a policymaker, you had a median projection and they heard you say you had a likely projection, they were receiving a materially different piece of information.

The executive summary used the word median correctly and consistently. It also, in one sentence, specified that the worst-case scenarios were in the appendix.

The sentence was: "Worst-case scenarios, defined as the 90th percentile outcomes, are available in the appendix and are not intended to be read as alarming but as the complete range of technically defensible projections."

He read this sentence several times.

"Not intended to be read as alarming but as the complete range of technically defensible projections."

That was a sentence written by someone who had thought about how it would be read. Who had understood that the people receiving the document would want to read it as alarming, or would want to avoid reading it as alarming, and who had made a specific choice about which of those risks to manage and how.

It was also a sentence that had not worked. The report had been reclassified. The people receiving it had managed the document rather than the risk it described.

He sat with this for a while.

He was not thinking about his grandfather. He was thinking about the sentence. The sentence and what it implied about the person who had written it: someone who had been careful, who had understood the institutional dynamics well enough to anticipate them, who had tried to thread a needle that could not be threaded.

Someone who had done everything correctly and watched it fail.

He added a note to his working document: see appendix for 90th percentile scenarios. He would need to look at these; they were directly relevant to his delay mechanism work, because the households in his dataset who had experienced the longest delays were in sub-zones where the actual outcomes had tracked the 90th percentile rather than the median.

He opened the appendix.

* * *

He finished at three in the afternoon.

He had read all two hundred and twelve pages, plus the appendix, which added thirty-one more. He had filled twelve pages of his working document with notes. He had found, in the course of reading, four methodological approaches he wanted to apply to his own dataset and two data sources he had not previously used that the study cited in its bibliography.

It was a good piece of work. That was the professional assessment, and it was accurate.

He closed the file.

He sat at his desk.

Through the window, the bay was doing the three-in-the-afternoon thing: the light past its midday flatness and beginning the long movement toward evening, the surface of the water catching it differently than it had in the morning.

He thought about the sentence in the executive summary. The needle that could not be threaded. The document that had been reclassified, that had circulated through institutional channels for six years before surfacing in a congressional disclosure, that had been accurate, that had predicted with forensic precision what had happened to a stretch of Gulf Coast that included a street where a house had stood for twenty-three years.

He thought about his grandfather on the deck of that house.

Not about what his grandfather had known or done or decided. Just the image: the posture, the hand on the railing, the quality of attention directed at the water. He had photographs of this posture. He had been watching it from the time he was old enough to notice anything.

He had been standing in that posture himself, last month, in the water of what had been that street.

He did not examine this further.

He saved his working document.

He closed the laptop.

He went to make coffee.

CHAPTER FIFTEEN:

Tampa, Florida · 2045

Priya had one more question.

He had submitted the revised delay mechanism section two days ago, incorporating the response to her earlier question about the specific event that moved a household from delay to departure. The revision had gone better than he expected; the mechanism was clearer now, the argument tighter, and he had found in the process of revising it that the prior knowledge indicator variable was doing more explanatory work than he had initially assigned it. He had expanded the discussion of this, and Priya had read it overnight, and now she was at his desk with the page in her hand and her single question.

"The prior knowledge indicator," she said. "You're treating it as a binary: household members with professional data access versus those without. But the data suggests something more granular. The length of time a household member has had access to the relevant data is at least as predictive as whether they had access at all."

He looked at her.

"The longer they've known," she said, "the longer they delay."

He took the page.

He sat with this for a moment. She was right; he could see it in the data now that she had named it. The variable was not binary. It was longitudinal. The delay was not simply a function of having information. It was a function of how long you had been inside the condition of having information you had not acted on.

"I'll recode it," he said.

She nodded and went back to her desk.

He looked at the page for a while before he opened the dataset.

* * *

The recoding took three days.

Not because the technical operation was complex; it was not. Because recoding a variable from binary to longitudinal required him to go back through all forty-seven entries in the mid-coastal cluster and, for the entries where the prior knowledge indicator was positive, establish when the relevant household member had first acquired the data access that qualified them for inclusion. This meant additional research for sixteen entries.

In the course of doing this research, he went back to the bibliography of the 2019 FDRA study.

He had looked at it when he first read the study, noting the sources the author had drawn on for the methodology and the projection modeling. He had added several of them to his own reading list. He now looked at it again more carefully, because the recoding work required him to understand not just when his grandfather had produced the study, but when he had first had access to the data that informed it, which was a different question.

The study cited modeling from the Dutch Deltares Institute for two of its sub-zone projections, specifically the sections on barrier island degradation rate and tidal inlet dynamics. He had used Deltares data in his own work; they were the leading hydrological research institute in the world for coastal flood modeling, and their datasets were widely cited. He pulled the specific Deltares studies cited in the 2019 FDRA report and found that the relevant datasets had been produced between 2016 and 2018.

His grandfather had had access to this data, through Deltares, from at least 2016.

He updated the entry in his dataset.

He did not examine what this number meant for the longitudinal variable. He moved to the next entry.

* * *

Two weeks later, he was expanding his literature review for the delay mechanism paper.

The recoding had strengthened the prior knowledge indicator variable significantly, and Priya had reviewed the updated analysis and said, with the quality of approval she reserved for things that had genuinely improved rather than merely changed, that the longitudinal framing was the right one and that the paper was now ready for the next stage, which was situating it in the broader international literature. He needed to review the recent displacement research from other contexts: what other countries had produced on informed delay patterns, whether the mechanism he had identified in the Gulf Coast corridor appeared elsewhere, what the comparative literature said.

He started with the Netherlands.

The Dutch displacement literature was the most developed in the world. The Netherlands had been managing climate-driven displacement research longer than anywhere else, with the advantage of a country that had been in an organized relationship with managed retreat for decades and had the institutional architecture to study it carefully. He had read some of this literature before. He now went deeper.

He found a body of work from Deltares that had appeared between 2031 and 2038, following the publication of what the literature referred to as the Delta Works re-assessment. He had been aware of this event in general terms; it had been significant enough in international climate policy circles that it was impossible to work in this space without knowing that the Netherlands had, in the early 2030s, published a reassessment of its flagship flood protection system that had been controversial, legally contested, and ultimately foundational to a decade of European climate infrastructure policy.

He had not previously engaged with the primary literature from this period.

He started reading.

* * *

The research was exceptional.

Not in a general sense; in the sense of work that had been done by someone who understood both the technical material and its human implications, and who had refused to let the technical rigor serve as a substitute for the human honesty. The Deltares papers from this period had a quality he recognized from his grandfather's 2019 study: the same refusal to hedge the confidence intervals, the same specificity about what the data did and did not support, the same plain language in the executive summaries that made the findings available to readers who were not specialists without sacrificing the precision that specialists required.

He read the lead author's name on several of the papers.

M. Van Der Berg, Deltares Institute, Rotterdam.

He noted this and kept reading.

The papers from 2031 to 2035 were the ones that interested him most, because they covered the period immediately following the Delta Works re-assessment publication, and they contained something he had not anticipated: a set of retrospective analyzes of the institutional history of the data, examining how the modeling had been produced, suppressed, eventually published, and received. These analyzes were not polemical; they were methodological, examining the specific mechanisms by which technically accurate data had been delayed in entering the public domain and what the consequences of that delay had been for infrastructure planning.

He had been building a dataset about exactly this mechanism in a different country.

He sat with this for a while.

Then he pulled the citation records for the 2031 Deltares papers to see what they had in turn cited.

* * *

The 2033 Van Der Berg paper on institutional delay in flood risk disclosure cited his grandfather's report.

Not prominently, it was one of fourteen international case studies in a comparative analysis of how governments in six countries had managed technically accurate flood risk data. The citation appeared in a footnote identifying the 2019 FDRA study as an early example of the pattern the paper was analyzing: a high-quality internal study, produced at significant professional cost, classified by political appointees, and circulated through institutional channels for years before entering the public record.

The footnote was four lines long.

He read it three times.

His grandfather's work had been cited in Rotterdam in 2033. In a paper about the specific mechanism by which technically accurate data was buried by institutions that found it inconvenient. In a paper written by someone who had been through a version of the same thing herself, in a different country, with a different engineering system, and who had made a different choice about what to do with the data she was holding.

He did not know the name M. Van Der Berg. He had no context for who this person was beyond the papers he had just read. He had no way of knowing, from the citation alone, whether the footnote represented a casual literature review or a specific knowledge of the 2019 FDRA study that went beyond the documentary record.

He added M. Van Der Berg to his bibliography.

He added a note: see also Van Der Berg (2033) for comparative international case study including this dataset.

He moved on.

* * *

He had a colleague in Dhaka.

Her name was Farah, and she worked for a climate migration research organization that had been operating in the Brahmaputra Delta since 2035. He had met her at a conference in 2042 and they had been in intermittent professional contact since, exchanging datasets and occasionally co-authoring short pieces for journals that covered the intersection of their work. She was four years older than him, precise and dry in her professional communications, and she had once sent him a dataset note that said only: "your Gulf Coast delay patterns mirror mine. call me." He had called her. They had talked for two hours.

He sent her an email.

He described what he had found in the comparative literature: the Van Der Berg papers, the Deltares retrospective analyzes, the pattern of informed institutional delay appearing across multiple national contexts in similar forms. He asked whether her Delta data showed the same longitudinal relationship between duration of prior knowledge and length of departure delay that he had found in his Gulf Coast dataset.

She replied within six hours, which was fast for Farah.

Her reply was three paragraphs. The first confirmed that yes, she was seeing the same pattern in the Delta data and had been for two years; she had not yet written it up in a form she was ready to share but was close. The second described the specific mechanism in the Delta context, which had a layer he had not encountered in his Gulf Coast data: the presence of institutional knowledge at a community level, where local engineers and surveyors had access to displacement data that they had not shared with the communities they were working in, for reasons that were sometimes institutional and sometimes personal. The third paragraph ended: "the architecture is the same everywhere. the geography changes. the silence is the same silence."

He saved the email.

He added her as a co-author note in his working document: data from T. Hossain / Dhaka Water Authority also cited in Delta context - follow up.

He paused.

He looked at the name he had typed.

T. Hossain. It was a common name in Bangladesh; he had encountered it in the literature before, in the context of Delta infrastructure work. He had no reason to associate it with anything specific. He had typed it from Farah's email, where she had cited a Dhaka Water Authority engineer whose data she was using in her own analysis.

He looked at it for a moment.

He changed the note to: Dhaka Water Authority, Delta corridor data - follow up via Farah.

He moved on.

* * *

The Arizona data was harder to find.

This was not unusual; the Southwest displacement literature was thinner than the coastal literature, partly because the displacement mechanism was different, groundwater depletion and temperature rather than inundation, and partly because the political context in Arizona had made institutional data sharing more difficult across the relevant period. He had a sub-dataset for the Sonoran corridor that he had built from public records and state filings, but it was less complete than his Gulf Coast data, and the prior knowledge indicator was harder to establish for households in this region because the relevant professional data had, in many cases, never entered the public record at all.

He found a DWR filing from 2031 that referenced an internal projection study that had apparently not been released publicly. The filing mentioned the study in the context of a policy review, citing it as the basis for a set of recommendations that the DWR had not implemented. He searched for the study. He could not find it.

He noted the gap in his working document and moved on.

The Arizona thread would need more work. He added it to his list of things to follow up when he had time.

* * *

He left later than usual.

The floor was empty by the time he closed his laptop. He had been inside the literature review for most of the day, reading and noting and following citations in the way that literary work sometimes pulled you from one thing to another until you looked up and the light through the window had changed completely.

He stood at his desk.

He had, in the course of a working day, moved from a single address in his Gulf Coast dataset to a set of related findings across three countries. His grandfather's report had been cited in Rotterdam. His longitudinal variable had a parallel in the Brahmaputra Delta. The Arizona data had a gap where a similar document should have been.

These were research findings. He would need to write them up, situate them in the paper, decide how much comparative framing the argument could support without losing its specificity to the Gulf Coast corridor. These were methodological decisions he would think through with Priya.

He put on his jacket.

He thought about the sentence in Farah's email: the architecture is the same everywhere. the geography changes. the silence is the same silence.

He had worked in this research space for seven years. He had known, as a professional matter, that the patterns he was studying were not unique to the Gulf Coast: the same mechanisms of informed delay, the same institutional dynamics around data suppression, the same human calculus of staying past the rational threshold. He had known this abstractly.

He knew it differently now.

He picked up his bag.

He stood at the window for a moment. The bay was dark, the evening complete, the lights of the city doing what they did from this angle, which was to make the water look purposeful rather than indifferent.

He went home.

He had a lot of work to do.

CHAPTER SIXTEEN:

Tampa, Florida · 2045

The paper was almost finished.

He had been working on it for eight months, from the first version of the delay mechanism section through the longitudinal recoding and the comparative literature review and the three subsequent revisions that Priya's questions had produced. The current draft was twenty-six pages, excluding references, and it was in the condition of a piece of work that had found its argument: where the sections fit each other correctly and the logic moved forward without requiring the reader to supply connections the author had not made. He had read it through twice in the past week and found it sound.

Priya had read it and said: ready.

He had one thing left to do before he submitted it.

* * *

The 2019 FDRA study appeared twice in his references.

The first citation was in the methodology section, where he had cited it as a prior instance of property-level inundation projection at the sub-zone scale. This was a technical citation; he was situating his own methodology in relation to existing approaches, and the 2019 study was directly relevant.

The second citation was in the comparative literature section, where he had noted the study as an example of institutional suppression of technically accurate flood risk data, alongside the Van Der Berg (2033) paper and two other international cases. This citation appeared in a paragraph that had grown, across revisions, into the paper's most substantive engagement with the institutional dimension of the problem.

Both citations listed the study correctly: Alderman, F. (2019). "Coastal Residential Obsolescence: A 30-Year Projection." Internal report, FDRA Regional Office. Reclassified 2019. Disclosed via congressional subcommittee, 2024.

He had been looking at these two citations for three weeks.

Not continuously, he had other work, other demands, the ordinary density of a working life. But they had been present in the way certain things were present: not requiring attention but available to it, surfacing reliably when other things cleared.

* * *

The citation was, professionally, entirely straightforward.

The 2019 FDRA study was a public record. It had been part of the congressional disclosure since 2024. It had been cited in at least fourteen subsequent studies, including the Van Der Berg (2033) paper. Citing it in a paper about informed delay and institutional suppression of flood risk data was not only appropriate but arguably necessary; it was one of the clearest documented cases of the mechanism he was describing.

There was no professional question about whether to cite it. The professional question had been answered before he began writing. The study was relevant. He was citing it.

What he had been sitting with for three weeks was a different question.

The different question was not about the citation. It was about what the citation did.

* * *

His grandfather's name would appear in his paper.

Not prominently, it was a reference entry and two in-text citations, the way a thousand names appeared in the references of any academic paper. A reader who was not looking for it would not notice it. A reader who happened to know the name would see it, and see it cited in a paper about why people who knew the data stayed past the rational threshold and draw whatever conclusion they drew.

He had not told anyone in his family what he had found. Not his mother, not his grandmother. He had found a document in August, and it was now April and in the intervening eight months he had read the document, recoded a variable, expanded a literature review, written a paper, and not mentioned any of this to the people it most directly concerned.

He was aware of the duration. He was aware that the duration itself was a kind of information.

He was also aware that what he was about to do - submit a paper that cited his grandfather's suppressed report in the context of a study of informed delay - was not the same thing as telling his family what he had found. It was not a family conversation. It was a professional publication. The two things were not the same.

He had been sitting with the space between them for three weeks.

* * *

His grandfather had known the data and stayed.

He had known what the data meant for the house he lived in, for the street, for the specific stretch of coast his family occupied. He had known this with forensic precision, had produced the forensic precision himself, and had lived inside it for twelve years without saying so.

Isaiah was not staying. He had not been in Coral Bay for four years before the house was gone, and he had left not because of a decision about data but because he had grown up inside a household that had been quietly, consistently, preparing its youngest member for departure. He had left the way water found its level: not because he chose to leave but because the direction was clear and he moved in the direction that was clear.

He was not his grandfather.

But he was sitting at his desk with a paper that cited his grandfather's report in the context of a study of why people did what his grandfather did, and the paper was almost ready to submit, and he had not told anyone in his family what it contained, and the eight months of not-telling had a specific quality he recognized.

He recognized it because he had grown up inside it.

This was the thing he had been sitting with.

* * *

He opened a new document.

He had done this before: opened a new document to think on the page rather than in his head, which was a habit he had developed in graduate school, and which worked for problems that were not resolving through thought alone. He typed the question he had been sitting with, stated plainly.

What is this citation for?

He looked at it.

The professional answer: it is a citation in an academic paper, supporting a claim about institutional suppression of flood risk data, for which it is directly relevant evidence.

The other answer, which was not a professional answer, was harder to state plainly. He tried.

It is a record that he existed. That he did the work. That the work was accurate. That the work was suppressed, and that its suppression had consequences that were documented and studied, and that someone has now put those consequences in a paper that will be read by people who study these things.

He looked at this for a while.

He had not, until he typed it, understood that this was what the citation was doing. He had been thinking of it as a methodological decision. It was also something else: an act of professional acknowledgement that was available to him in a way that a family conversation was not, and that his grandfather's work would not receive from any other direction, because the report had been reclassified and the institution that had reclassified it had no mechanism for retroactive recognition of the thing it had buried.

He closed the new document without saving it.

* * *

He sat at his desk for a long time.

The bay went through its evening sequence outside the window: the gold developing and then deepening and then beginning the shift toward the flat dark of full night, the lights on the water multiplying as the sky dimmed. He had watched this sequence many times from this window. It was reliable in the way that certain things were reliable.

He thought about Priya's sentence: the longer they've known, the longer they delay. He had recoded the variable on the basis of this insight and the variable had become more predictive. His grandfather had known for twelve years. He had known for eight months. The durations were not comparable. But the structure was the same structure.

He thought about whether that meant he should submit the paper or not submit it.

He thought about this carefully.

It did not mean he should not submit it. The paper was sound. The citation was appropriate. The work his grandfather had done deserved to be in the record, correctly attributed, as part of the documented history of how this mechanism had operated. Not citing it, now that he had found it, would be a different kind of choice: the choice to keep the document out of his paper because of what it was to him personally, which was a choice that would compromise his research rather than protect his family.

His family was not in need of protection from this. The house was gone. His grandfather was gone. His mother and grandmother knew what had happened; they had been sitting with it longer than he had. The paper was not news to them, even if they did not know the paper existed.

He was not his grandfather.

He thought about this for a while.

He thought about what it would mean to submit the paper and then call his mother. Not to tell her he was about to publish something that cited his grandfather's report; he would not frame it that way. But to call her, in the general sense, because he had not spoken to her in two weeks and there was a kind of distance that accumulated when you were inside a piece of work and did not speak to the people you were close to, and he had been inside this piece of work for eight months.

He thought about calling his grandmother.

He had not called her in longer than two weeks. She was seventy-nine. She was sharp and economical in conversation and had the quality of people who had survived a great deal: a complete absence of interest in managing how things appeared. She said what was true. She received what was true. He had always found this restful.

He thought he might call her this week.

* * *

He opened the paper.

He read through the references section. Both citations were there, correctly formatted, correctly placed. The first in the methodology section, the second in the comparative literature paragraph.

The comparative literature paragraph read, in its final form: "The institutional suppression of technically accurate flood risk data has been documented across multiple national contexts. Cases include the 2019 FDRA internal study on Gulf Coast residential inundation (Alderman 2019), the Delta Works re-assessment in the Netherlands (Van Der Berg et al. 2031), and the Arizona DWR internal modeling referenced but not released in state filings from the same period. In each case, the suppression mechanism involved the intersection of professional data access, institutional authority, and the specific political calculus of disclosures whose accuracy could not be disputed but whose implications were considered unmanageable."

He read this paragraph twice.

It was accurate. It was the right paragraph in the right place. It did the work the paper needed it to do.

He moved his cursor to the submission portal.

He stopped.

Not from uncertainty about the paper; the paper was ready. From a quality of attention he wanted to bring to the act of submitting it. He had been inside this material for eight months. He had found something he had not expected to find, and he had moved around it for months in the way his household had taught him to move around things that were present but not named, and he had built it into a piece of work he believed in, and he was about to submit it.

He wanted to be present for the submission in the way you were present for things that mattered, which was simply to know what you were doing and why, without ceremony.

He knew what he was doing.

He knew why.

He moved his cursor back to the document.

He read the opening paragraph of the paper one final time.

Then he saved it.

He closed the laptop.

He would submit it in the morning.

He went to call his grandmother.

CHAPTER SEVENTEEN:

Florida: Tampa · 2045 / Coral Bay · 2031

His mother had asked him to go through a box.

Not a specific box; there were several, stacked in the spare room of her house in Tallahassee that had been accumulating since the move from the last Coral Bay house in 2036. She had been meaning to sort them for years and had not sorted them, and when he had been visiting in February, she had said: whenever you have time, if you wanted to help, there are papers in the spare room that probably have things that should go to your grandmother.

He had not had time in February. He had made time in April, the week before the paper was due, because making time for a concrete task was the kind of rest he needed when he was in the final stage of a piece of work and his mind would not stop running the argument.

He had been in the spare room for two hours.

Most of what he had found was administrative: insurance documents, property records, the detritus of four house moves across sixteen years, envelopes containing receipts from contractors whose names he did not recognize. He had sorted these into three piles: keep, discard, query. The query pile was for things he could not evaluate without knowing more about their context, and it had grown to a height he was not entirely comfortable with.

He found the envelope at the bottom of the third box.

It was a standard white envelope, sealed, with his grandmother's handwriting on the front. Not addressed, just a name. Frank.

He held it for a moment.

Then he opened it.

* * *

The letter was three pages, handwritten on the cream notepaper his grandmother kept in the desk drawer in the kitchen.

He knew this notepaper; he had seen her write on it for as long as he could remember. She used it for the letters she still wrote by hand to people she considered deserved the specific attention of handwriting, which was a category she had not explained to him but which he understood, from the recipients he had observed over the years, to have its own internal logic.

He sat on the floor of the spare room and read it.

Frank,

I don't know if I'm going to send this. I've been sitting at the kitchen table for an hour trying to decide. That's probably the answer.

Deja told me on Wednesday. I've been going back and forward since then between wanting to talk to you and not being able to find the right thing to say, and I think writing it down is the only way I'm going to know what the right thing is.

I'm not angry. I want to say that first because I know you're expecting anger and I think that's making it harder for you to be in the same room with me, which I've noticed. What I feel is more like - I keep thinking of that word, disoriented. I've been disoriented since Wednesday. Not because the information is new, exactly. Because having a name for it is new.

I knew something was wrong. I want to be honest about that. I've known it for years - I couldn't have told you what it was, but I knew it was there, in the way you looked at the water, in the way you built the drainage in the garage that summer I was in Tallahassee. You thought I didn't notice that you did it while I was away. I noticed. I decided not to ask about it.

That's the part I've been sitting with since Wednesday. I decided not to ask. I told myself I was giving you time, or that you'd tell me when you were ready, or that it was your professional business and I shouldn't press. But those weren't the real reasons. The real reason was that I was afraid of what the answer would require me to do with it. I had a life I loved in that house. I loved it honestly. I didn't want to know something that would make me love it differently.

So, I chose not to know. Twelve years. I managed what I asked and what I didn't ask. I kept the evenings livable. I don't think you knew I was doing this. I think you thought I simply didn't see it. I saw it. I looked at it from a distance, and I filed it and I kept going.

I don't know if that was love, or cowardice. I've been thinking about this all week. I keep arriving at the same answer, which is: I think it was both. I think most love is.

What I want to say to you - and I don't know if I'll say it out loud, that's why I'm writing it down - is that I'm not asking you to explain the twelve years. I know the shape of them. I know why you stayed. I understand the report and I understand the reclassification and I understand why the right moment never arrived, because I was helping it not arrive, and that is something I have to sit with.

What I'm asking - and I think this is what I want, though I'm not entirely sure - is for us to stop being careful. I don't want to manage the evenings anymore. I don't want to offer you the easier sentence when I have the harder one in my mouth. I'm sixty-eight years old and I'm tired of the particular kind of attention it takes to know something without saying you know it.

I put the folder on the shelf because I wanted it to be visible. Not as a punishment. As a fact. This is a thing that is part of our life now, like the ceramic bowl and the photograph of my mother. I'm not putting it away. I'm not pretending it's not there. I don't know what I'm going to do with it, but it's going to be where I can see it.

I think you stayed because leaving would have meant admitting that the life we built was built on something you couldn't fix. I understand this better than you might think. I stayed in not-knowing because not-knowing was a way of protecting the same life. We were protecting the same thing, Frank. We just made different choices about how to do it.

I don't know if that makes it better or worse. I've been going back and forward on this too.

I love you. That's not the complicated part. The complicated part is that love didn't stop any of this from happening, and I'm not sure I know what that means yet.

I'm going to make dinner now. I might give you this letter. I might not.

Gloria

* * *

He sat on the floor of the spare room for a long time.

The box was open beside him. The other papers were in their three piles. The envelope was in his hands.

He read it twice. Not because it was unclear; because the first reading had produced something he needed to read through again before he could determine what it was.

His grandmother had written this in 2031. She had been sixty-eight. She had sat at the kitchen table after Deja told her and she had written three pages on the cream notepaper and sealed the envelope and addressed it to his grandfather and then not sent it. He did not know where it had been between 2031 and now: in the kitchen desk, in a box when they moved, in his mother's spare room. He did not know if his grandfather had ever seen it. He did not know if his grandmother had intended anyone else to find it.

He thought about calling her.

He thought about what he would say. He had been planning to call her this week anyway, in the general sense of having been away from family contact for too long and needing to correct this. He could call her and ask whether she knew this letter was in a box in Tallahassee. He could ask whether she wanted it back.

He thought about this.

She would probably say: keep it, if you want it. Or: throw it away, it doesn't matter now. She had the distinct trait, which he had always found both restful and occasionally startling, of not being attached to the management of her own history. She said what was true and received what was true and did not, as far as he had observed, spend much energy on the question of how things appeared.

She had known. She had decided what she needed to know. She had named this, in the letter, without flinching from what naming it meant.

He sat with this.

* * *

He had spent eight months moving around his grandfather's name in his dataset.

He had recoded variables and expanded literature reviews and written a paper that was sitting on his laptop ready to submit in the morning. He had done this work carefully and he believed in it and he was going to submit it. None of that had changed.

What the letter changed was something else: his understanding of what the household had been.

He had grown up inside a household organized around something unnamed, and he had understood this as his grandfather's architecture: the private knowledge, the managed evenings, the exacting care with which certain subjects were approached and then left. He had inherited the grammar of it without knowing where the grammar came from, and he had assumed it came from one direction.

It had come from both.

His grandmother had known the shape of it. She had been managing the not-knowing deliberately, for her own reasons, which were not cowardice and not ignorance but the deliberate calculation of a woman who understood what she was protecting and had chosen to protect it at a cost she had not fully accounted for until she sat at a kitchen table on a Wednesday in 2031 and wrote a letter she did not send.

"I think it was both. I think most love is."

He had not expected to find this sentence in a box in Tallahassee. He had not expected it to be the sentence that clarified something he had been trying to understand for eight months.

He put the letter back in the envelope.

He put the envelope in the keep pile.

* * *

He called his grandmother that evening.

Not about the letter. He did not mention the letter. He called because he had been meaning to call and because the specific quality of sitting on the floor of his mother's spare room with an unsent letter in his hands had made him want to hear her voice in the ordinary sense, the way you sometimes wanted a thing more specifically after being close to its absence.

She answered on the third ring.

"Isaiah," she said, with the familiar warmth she had always brought to his name: a mild pleasure, no performance.

"Hi Grandma."

"Where are you?"

"Tallahassee. Helping Mum with some boxes."

"How is she?"

"Good. Busy."

"And you? You sound like you're inside something."

He paused. "I'm finishing a paper."

"Mm." The specific sound she made when she was neither accepting nor rejecting an explanation, simply noting it. "Is it good work?"

"I think so."

"Then it's worth being inside."

He sat with this for a moment.

"How are you?" he said.

"Fine," she said. "The garden is doing something peculiar with the tomatoes. I'm watching it with interest."

He almost said: I found a letter in a box here. He did not say it. Not because it was not available to be said, but because it did not need to be said tonight, and he had learned, or was learning, the difference between the things that needed to be said and the things that were simply present.

They talked for twenty minutes. About the tomatoes. About his sister Amara, who had moved to Atlanta and was doing something in urban planning that Gloria found interesting and slightly mysterious. About nothing in particular, in the way that the conversations that mattered were often about nothing in particular.

When they said goodnight, she said: "Come and visit when you're out of the paper."

"I will," he said.

"Good," she said. And hung up.

He sat in the spare room a while longer.

The boxes were sorted. The keep pile had the envelope in it. Tomorrow he would submit the paper.

He thought about his grandmother in her kitchen with the cream notepaper and the thing she had decided what to do with.

He thought about what it cost to know something and keep going anyway.

He turned off the light.

He went to sleep.

CHAPTER EIGHTEEN:

Tampa, Florida · 2045

He submitted the paper at eight-seventeen in the morning.

He had been at his desk since seven-thirty, which was earlier than his usual start. He had made coffee, opened the laptop, and read through the paper one final time: not looking for errors, which he had addressed in the previous week's revisions, but for the quality of readiness that he had learned to trust over seven years of research work. The paper was ready. He had known it was ready yesterday and he knew it now.

He moved his cursor to the submission portal.

The journal was one of the three he and Priya had identified as appropriate for this work: field-specific, rigorous, the right readership for what the paper was arguing. The submission process was standard: upload the manuscript, the data supplement, the acknowledgements. Confirm the corresponding author. Click submit.

He clicked submit.

The confirmation appeared on his screen: Manuscript received. Reference number assigned. You will be notified of the editorial decision within sixty to ninety days.

He looked at the confirmation for a moment.

Then he closed the portal.

* * *

He opened the paper one more time.

He went to the references section. He read through it: forty-three citations, listed alphabetically by author. He found the two entries for the 2019 FDRA study, where he had expected to find them.

Alderman, F. (2019). "Coastal Residential Obsolescence: A 30-Year Projection." Internal report, FDRA Regional Office. Reclassified 2019. Disclosed via congressional subcommittee, 2024.

He read his grandfather's name in the reference list of a published academic paper. Not published yet; it would be sixty to ninety days before editorial decision. But submitted. In the system. Available to the reviewers who would read it, and, if accepted, to everyone who subsequently read the paper or followed its citations.

His grandfather had produced a piece of work in 2019. It had been reclassified. It had circulated through institutional channels and eventually surfaced in a congressional disclosure. It had been cited in a Dutch paper about institutional suppression of flood risk data. It was now cited in his paper about the specific mechanisms of informed delay, as both a methodological precedent and a documented case of the pattern he was analyzing.

The work was in the record.

Not as a memorial. Not as a gesture. As a citation: specific, attributed, part of the documented evidence base for a field of study that did not exist as a field when the work was produced. His grandfather had been right about what he found. He had been right about the projections, right about the confidence intervals, right about the timeline. The work deserved to be cited. Isaiah had cited it.

This was the sum of what he had done.

He closed the laptop.

* * *

Priya arrived at nine.

She put her bag down and looked at him with the intent attention she brought to the mornings after a significant piece of work had been completed: not celebratory, simply noting.

"Submitted?"

"Yes."

She nodded. "Good." She took off her jacket and hung it on her chair. "I have comments on the Farah co-authorship proposal when you're ready. No rush today."

"I'm ready," he said.

She looked at him again. "Take the morning."

He considered arguing. He did not argue. Priya's instructions about his own capacity were generally more accurate than his own.

"All right," he said.

She sat at her desk.

He looked at his laptop, closed on the desk in front of him.

He thought about what to do with a morning that did not have the paper in it. The answer did not come immediately. This was, he understood, the disorientation of a piece of work ending: the space it occupied did not know yet what to become.

He thought about going for a walk.

* * *

He walked south along the waterfront.

The bay in the morning was different from the bay in the afternoon or the evening: flatter, the light younger, the water a different quality of gray-green that would shift over the course of the day toward the blues and silvers of afternoon. He had been watching this water for three years from his desk window and had walked along it many times, but mornings were rarer; he was usually at his desk by this hour.

He walked without a destination. This was not his usual mode; he was a person who moved between places rather than through them, who understood walking as transit rather than as the thing itself. Today he was walking as the thing itself. He was not entirely sure what that meant but he was willing to find out.

The path along the waterfront was mostly empty at this hour. A few runners. A man with a dog moving through the specific unhurried attention of a person whose morning schedule was organized around the dog's preferences rather than his own. A woman in a yellow jacket sitting on a bench looking at the water.

He walked.

* * *

He thought about his grandfather.

Not in a directed way; just the fact of him, the way you thought about people who were gone when the thinking was available rather than deliberate. His grandfather had been a man who watched water. Who built things that lasted. Who carried something for forty years and did not put it down until it was taken from him, and then had stood in the kitchen of his own house, emptied, not knowing what kind of man he was without the weight.

He had died at seventy-five. Isaiah had been at a field site in Louisiana and had driven back and sat in a room with his mother and grandmother. He had said the things that were available to be said. He had not known, then, what he knew now: that his grandfather's name was in a congressional disclosure, that his report was cited in Rotterdam, that the work had outlasted the institutional decision to bury it.

He did not know if his grandfather would have wanted to know this.

He thought he might have. He thought a man who had spent thirty years trying to make information legible to people who needed it would have found something in the knowledge that the information had eventually found its way into the record, where it could be read and cited and built on by people who came after. But he did not know. He had not known his grandfather well enough to know what he would have wanted, which was a specific gap in his understanding that he had been aware of for years and that he was now, after nine months of reading his grandfather's work, aware of differently.

He walked past a heron standing at the water's edge.

The heron did not move. It was doing what herons did: reading the water with the complete and unhurried attention of a creature for whom this was the entire task.

He had watched herons do this from the deck of the Coral Bay house when he was a child. He had watched his grandfather do it too, in a different register, with a different instrument.

He kept walking.

* * *

He thought about his grandmother's letter.

He had put it in the keep pile. He would bring it back to Tampa with him and put it somewhere he could find it if he needed to find it, which he did not know yet whether he would. He had not decided what to do with it in a larger sense, and he understood that the not-deciding was itself a position: he was letting it be present without requiring it to become anything specific yet, which was a thing he had learned, or was learning, to do.

His grandmother had written: I think it was both. I think most love is.

He had been turning this over since the spare room in Tallahassee. Not because it clarified something he had been confused about; he had not been confused about his grandparents' marriage, exactly. Because it named something he had been aware of without having a name for: the way that love and the failures of love were not separate things but the same thing seen from different angles, and that the angle you were standing at depended on what you were trying to protect.

He did not know if he had fully understood this.

He knew he was walking with it.

* * *

He had three projects in various stages of development.

The co-authorship proposal with Farah, which Priya had comments on and which he would read this afternoon. A follow-up question from the delay mechanism paper: whether the longitudinal variable behaved differently in households where the suppression of data had been institutional rather than personal, which was a distinction his Gulf Coast dataset did not capture cleanly but which the Deltares retrospective literature might illuminate. And a request from a colleague in Phoenix who was working on the Arizona corridor data, who had asked whether Isaiah's prior knowledge indicator methodology was transferable to a context where the data suppression had been administrative rather than professional.

He would respond to all three. The work continued; this was the nature of research, that each question produced the next question, that the paper you submitted was also the beginning of what came after it.

He did not find this discouraging.

He had chosen this work because the questions it asked were questions that mattered, and the questions that mattered did not resolve, they accumulated, and the accumulation was the work. He was twenty-nine. He had been doing this for seven years and he expected to keep doing it for a long time.

His grandfather had done it for thirty years and watched the institutions fail to act on what he found.

He was not his grandfather.

He was also not not his grandfather.

He walked.

* * *

He reached the end of the waterfront path.

There was a small park here, a triangle of grass between the path and the road, with two benches and a tree that had been planted recently enough that it was still staked, the support poles at three angles holding it upright while it found its own. He sat on one of the benches.

The bay was in front of him. The morning light was doing what it did at this hour in April, which was to be clear and specific and without the heat that would come later. A pelican was moving along the waterline at the far edge of his vision, low and deliberate, the way pelicans moved when they were in the business of the morning rather than demonstrating anything.

He thought - in sixty to ninety days the paper will have an editorial decision.

He thought - I need to call my mother.

He thought - the heron was still at the water when I passed it.

These thoughts arrived without sequence, without the connective tissue that turned thoughts into argument. He let them arrive. He was not inside a piece of work at the moment. He was on a bench in a park in the morning, watching the water and the pelican and the light, which were doing what they did.

His notebook was in his jacket pocket.

He did not take it out.

He sat for a while.

Then he stood.

He put his hands in his pockets.

He walked back toward the Institute.

He had work to do.

AUTHOR'S NOTE

This novel began with a question, rather than a position.

I wanted to understand what happens when knowledge arrives long before action does; how people live alongside information they cannot yet use; and how silence, once chosen, becomes a structure that others grow up inside.

The events and institutions in this book are fictional. The patterns are not. They reflect situations I have encountered across different domains: in public institutions, in professional settings, and in families trying to protect what they have built while the ground beneath them shifts.

I have tried to write this novel without urgency, spectacle, or explanation. Not because the stakes are low, but because they are persistent. The damage it describes is slow. The choices are ordinary. Their consequences accumulate.

If the book resists closure, that is intentional. Some forms of knowledge do not resolve - they accompany. What matters, in the end, is not what is known, but how people move while carrying it.

\- *Jacob E. Williams*

www.ingramcontent.com/pod-product-compliance
Lightning Source LLC
LaVergne TN
LVHW020717110826
845149LV00012B/2304

* 9 7 9 8 9 9 5 7 0 0 4 0 1 *